THE SIXTH RAID

In the sixth raid, a cop was gunned down and a girl kidnapped. A bank clerk drew a likeness that matched police photographs of Brad Tolman — 'King of the Blaggers'. Julian Arbor, master of disguise, had carried out five consecutive raids on small branch banks. When the sixth raid came, Arbor was certain that Tolman must now be the sole suspect for them all. The top brass at Police Headquarters held the same view — but not Sam Bawtry, who decided to set a double trap . . .

Books by Douglas Enefer
in the Linford Mystery Library:

THE DEADLY STREAK
THE LAST LEAP

DOUGLAS ENEFER

THE
SIXTH RAID

Complete and Unabridged

LINFORD
Leicester

First published in Great Britain in 1979 by
Robert Hale Limited
London

First Linford Edition
published 1998
by arrangement with
Robert Hale Limited
London

British Library CIP Data

Enefer, Douglas, *1906*–
    The sixth raid.—Large print ed.—
Linford mystery library
    1. Detective and mystery stories
    2. Large type books
    I. Title
    823.9′14 [F]

ISBN 0–7089–5348–4

5 01086110

Published by
F. A. Thorpe (Publishing) Ltd.
Anstey, Leicestershire

Set by Words & Graphics Ltd.
Anstey, Leicestershire
Printed and bound in Great Britain by
T. J. International Ltd., Padstow, Cornwall

This book is printed on acid-free paper

1

The bank was in a side street almost within sight of the Salthouse and Albert docks. A small branch bank, which was one reason why he had chosen it; the other reason was that it had only just opened and he knew, from discreet watching, that at this hour the first customers had yet to turn up.

He was of average height, well dressed without ostentation, aged anywhere between thirty and forty, with thick ash-blond hair showing tentative streaks of grey and was wearing gold-rimmed spectacles. A small puckered scar on the left side of his face showed whitely against a light tan which suggested that he had lately been on holiday in the sun.

It was 9.32 on the morning of May 11. A clear warm day with a light breeze riffling in from the broad sweep of the river cleaving between Liverpool and the Wirral coast.

Margaret Higham, a pretty girl with a mass of chestnut hair, looked up as he came to her window.

'Nice day,' he said pleasantly.

'Yes, it is.' She smiled, not deliberately but because smiling came readily to her. 'Makes you feel good to be alive.'

He leaned forward slightly and said: 'If you want to stay that way just do exactly what I tell you.'

She went rigid.

'There's probably an alarm button on your side of the counter, but I wouldn't touch it if I were you.' He had a gun out, a .44 Colt automatic with a long silencer. 'Pretend you're dealing with a normal customer and stuff all the money you have available in this.' He slid a soft leather sack towards her. 'Quickly, now!'

He screened the gun with his swung-open jacket, but it was still looking at her. The back of her mouth felt grittily dry, so that it was a small physical pain even to swallow.

She opened a drawer. There was money in it; stacks of tens and fives. She put the

2

money in the sack, her frightened eyes still on the gun.

'More,' he said softly. 'Try the next drawer.'

She did what he said, but she had to change her position. A young male clerk at the other end of the counter noticed the movement and started towards them.

The ash-blond man waited for him to come close, then said tightly: 'I have a gun. You wouldn't want it to go off, not at this charming young lady — would you?'

Freddie Collins stopped moving. Everything he had ever mentally rehearsed about how to tackle a bank hold-up swam impotently in his mind, nullified by the stark reality of the gun. The man pulled the sack towards him. He grinned, aiming the gun as he walked backwards. He risked a fast glance over his shoulder. No one was coming in from the street. He shouldered one of the twin swing doors open and went through it, fast now. The bank was on a corner. He rounded it to where he had left a nondescript bicycle. In another moment he was riding it into Park Lane, on into St. James Street, then left on Upper Parliament Street and left again on Catherine Street, making for the Liverpool 8 district. Nobody would be looking for a bank raider on a bicycle.

A little short of Myrtle Street he propped the bicycle against the flaking front of what had once been a gentleman's town residence and walked away. Within minutes any one of half a hundred kids, black or white, would take the bike, which was what he wanted.

He turned left again, going towards Renshaw Street and Central Station. He spent ten minutes locked in a public lavatory and when he came out his face had no tan and no scar and he wasn't wearing glasses or thick ash-blond hair. He strolled to where he had parked his car, an L registration Escort.

By now the alarm would have been raised and his description given, but nobody would be looking for a man like him . . .

* * *

4

Brooker was alone in the big C.I.D. room smoking one of his small cigars. When he came in three d-cs were crouched over massive typewriters in the penultimate stages of composing reports with nicotine-stained index fingers. But one by one they drifted out, thankfully, because working under the bleak gaze of the Detective Chief Inspector tended to make them apprehensive; even the most self-possessed of the many detectives on the strength got an irrational feeling of guilt in his presence.

At fifty-four, with a leathery face and hard blue eyes, Brooker was generally conceded to be the toughest operator in the Merseyside Metropolitan Police. Even his superiors tended to regard him with a certain reserve. Only Sam Bawtry had achieved personal friendship, though there had been a time when the two men hadn't always got along — until the night when, out of the blue, Brooker had confided the facts of his ruined marriage.

It was common knowledge, though never so much as hinted at in his presence, that Marion Brooker had walked out on him, going off to London with a fella in the shipping business, a well known skirt-chaser, all teeth and implied virility. Then came the night when Brooker told Bawtry everything, and an unspoken *rapport* had grown up between the two. There were still occasional moments of mutual edginess, particularly when Bawtry was playing one of his lone hands, but the occasions were less frequent. Also, Brooker's irascibility had been softened privately by an affair, now more than a year old, with Joyce Wetherby, a small good-looking widow who lived out at Sefton Park in a paid-for bungalow on the money left by her husband, who died from a massive coronary after years of working and playing a shade too hard.

What Joyce saw in him baffled Brooker, who was no oil painting, and he had said as much to her. Joyce summed it up by saying: 'Brook — the short answer is that we're good for each other.' And this was true. Each attracted the other in a fusing of physical needs.

When Marion left him he had sat alone at night in the house out at Knotty Ash they had shared for twelve years, waiting for the telephone to ring or the sound of her key in the lock. It never happened. He stayed on there because he liked the house, keeping it in meticulous order and tending to his roses on his days off. Other nights, when he finished duty, he went out drinking, increasingly staying late at the Press Club. Until Marion went he hadn't been much of a drinking man but now he was, though nobody had ever seen him even half-cut or denied his implacable resolution as a cop.

For months after Marion quit he pondered what he would do if she came back. But she never did and the memory of their life together ebbed and he knew now that he didn't want her back. Nor was this solely because of Joyce, who didn't want another marriage any more than he did.

The thoughts were running through his mind when Bawtry walked in.

Brooker looked up with a welcoming

grin. 'Hi, Sam — everything under control?'

'Yes and no.'

'What's that mean?'

'Inquiries are under control, but we don't seem to be getting anywhere. Five bank raids in as many days and if there's a clue I haven't encountered it.'

'We will, we always do in the end. Well, happen not always — but mostly.'

Bawtry fought a losing battle with the desire for the first cigarette of the day. A former forty-a-day man, he had cut it down to twelve and was aiming, not optimistically, at ten. He lit one, dragging gratefully, and went on: 'A score of d-cs, plus the uniformed mob, have chatted-up all the Neds on the patch. So far as can be assessed, they're all clean.'

Brooker eyed his Detective Inspector thoughtfully. 'Could be a new lot, not necessarily Scousers. A new lot moving into Liverpool.' Brooker shifted in his chair, tipping the front legs off the floor. 'Did you get on the blower to Manchester and London?'

Sam nodded. 'Also several other cities.

I drew blanks all round. No reports of villains heading for Liverpool, or anywhere else if it comes to that.'

'Any ideas of your own?'

'Nothing worth telling.'

'Everything's worth telling.' Brooker's mouth began to tighten. 'You're not keeping something back, are you, Sam?'

'No.' For a moment Bawtry felt the old edginess coming on. Then he smiled and said: 'My thoughts match yours. I mean the theory that a new mob may be working here. It's the only one that fits.'

'That's a fact. All five raids carried out by men of widely different appearance. It's too much to suppose that they're working independently of each other. My guess is a gang, each member taking turns in the actual hold-ups while one or more of the others acts as look-out.' Brooker mashed out the splayed end of his small cigar. 'We'd better get a lead soon if we don't want the Chief Con breathing down our necks . . . ' He broke off as Jenny Mycroft walked in from Information Control. 'Yes, Jenny?'

9

'Another bank raid just reported.'

'God Almighty, not *again*?'

'You don't need to call on your Maker, Mr. Brooker,' said Jenny Mycroft primly.

'Why not? We need all the help we can get. Any details?'

'Same technique — one man, armed, entered the bank immediately after it opened. The Allied Mercantile Bank in Lexton Street. By the time the staff got to the front door he had gone — with £7,567.'

'Have we got anyone there?'

'Not yet. I've only just got the message. The manager rang through.'

Brooker picked up his hat. 'Is there a squad car available?'

'One's just coming in, Constable Armiston driving.'

'We'll go in that,' said Brooker.

2

The manager came forward as they went into the bank. Charles Anson, a stocky rubicund man in his fifties.

'Miss Higham is in my office with her doctor. I judged it best to send for him . . . ' he began.

'It was her section this fella went to?'

'Yes. She wasn't hurt physically, but she's in a state of shock. Understandable in the circumstances.' He led the way in. The doctor glanced up.

'Police?'

Brooker said who they were. 'How is this young lady?'

'She'll be all right. I've given her a tranquiliser.'

'Can we talk to her?'

'Oh, yes, that'll be all right. Try to keep it brief, perhaps.'

Margaret Higham, who was sitting in the manager's leather chair, smiled faintly. 'I'm a little better now.'

11

Two uniformed constables arrived, Brooker looked sideways at Bawtry, a silent signal.

Sam said: 'The man who held you up, Miss Higham — can you describe him accurately?'

'I think so. About five foot nine, average build with ash-blond hair, rather thick and starting to go grey at the sides. He looked as if he could have been on holiday, Spain or somewhere like that. I mean he had a tan, not a deep tan but more than you'd expect in England at this time of year.'

'His accent?'

'Not Liverpool — more like Manchester, I'd say, though I can't be positive . . . ' She hesitated.

'Has something occurred to you, Miss Higham?'

'I'm not sure. What I mean is I got the impression it might not be genuine.'

'You thought he was putting on a Manchester voice, is that what you mean?'

'I can't be certain, but I did think that, yes.'

'Why?'

'The accent didn't seem to go with his appearance. He was well-dressed in a quiet sort of way. I mean he looked like an educated man who probably wouldn't have a pronounced accent.' She pushed a strand of hair off the side of her oval face. 'I hope that doesn't sound snobby . . . '

Bawtry smiled. 'More a tribute to your powers of observation, Miss Higham. Anything else?'

'I noticed that he had a white scar on the left side of his face, high up near the temple. Oh, and he was wearing tinted glasses, gold-rimmed ones.'

'Tell us exactly what happened, the way it happened, Miss Higham.'

She folded her hands in her lap. They were still trembling slightly, but her voice was composed. She went through it, in sequence and not muddling fact with opinion.

Bawtry said quietly: 'You'll make a good witness if we catch this man.'

'*When* you catch him, Inspector,' said Anson.

'I hope you're right, sir. By the time

members of your staff got out of the bank this fella had disappeared?'

'Unfortunately, yes.' The manager palmed a hand over thinning hair. 'A point — I don't think he had a car.'

'You didn't hear one start up, you mean?'

'No, and we would have heard — it's quiet round here at nine-thirty in the morning.'

'How many minutes elapsed before you or your staff ran out of the bank?'

'A minute, two at the most. Collins, one of the staff, saw what happened and shouted to me and I followed him out into the street, but the man had gone.'

'You don't know which way he went?'

'I can't say for certain. He could've run down into Shaws Alley, or gone the other way into Park Lane. The latter, I think — though that's just an opinion.'

Brooker said slowly: 'No getaway car, yet he's able to vanish in not much more'n a minute. It fits.'

The manager stared, not comprehending. Brooker smiled thinly. 'There's been five bank raids in as many days.

Each one took place at about the same time and in every case the fella got away quickly — yet apparently without using a car.'

'Unusual, isn't it?'

'Yes, it is.'

Margaret Higham looked from one to the other. 'I always thought bank raiders used stolen cars to get away fast.'

'As a rule, yes. We seem to be up against an unusual operator.'

Bawtry fingered his plain gold cufflinks. It was an unconscious mannerism with him, like Brooker's habit of jingling coins in his trousers pocket. 'It would take him a shade longer to get to Shaws Alley. I'd say, like Mr. Anson, that he made for Park Lane. Even that'd take a minute or so — yet you didn't see him. It was the same in the other raids . . . ' Bawtry paused.

'Yes, Sam?' said Brooker gently.

'It sounds daft — but he could've been riding a bicycle.'

Margaret laughed. 'A bank robber on a pedal bike! They always have a car. Well, on television, anyway.'

Brooker grinned. 'This isn't television. You may be right, Sam — nobody'd be looking for a villain riding a bike. You didn't see a cyclist, by any chance?' This to Anson.

The manager shook his head. 'No, but as you suggest, no one would be looking for a man on a bicycle. It's possible there was one, but I didn't notice.'

'The four other incidents were all similar in execution. A man enters the premises, holds up the counter clerk, makes off with a bag or sack of money and by the time the staff get outside he's gone. Mind you, he could've had one or more accomplices hanging about outside the bank on the lookout, but they could pass as ordinary members of the public.'

'The description Miss Higham gave you of this man — does it fit any of the others?'

'No, they were all different in appearance. Could be a gang taking turns on a prearranged system. We'll try to find out.' Brooker drove hands into his pockets. 'Thank you for your help, Miss

16

Higham — you, too, sir. A constable will take statements from you, also from Mr. Collins here. We'll be in touch.'

The squad car took them back to Headquarters. A lone d-c said: 'The Detective Chief Super wants to see you, Mr. Brooker. You as well, Mr. Bawtry.'

They crossed the courtyard and went into the office jointly shared by Detective Chief Superintendent Braxted and Detective Superintendent Fallon.

'Well?' Braxted fired the question, drumming well-tended fingers on the wide desk. The action implied the onset of slight irascibility.

Brooker took a seat and said evenly: 'We haven't felt a collar yet.'

'I hardly expected you to bring him back with you, Brooker.' Braxted reached for the internal telephone. 'Ballinger wants to hear your story.'

Herbert Dalton Ballinger was one of the two Assistant Chief Constables, a lithe, compact man with the bearing of an Army officer. He had gone from cadet college to junior commissioned rank, winding up as a brigadier with some fairly tough overseas service before joining the police at the age of fifty.

When he came in he said: 'Morning, Brooker. You, too, Bawtry.' He had a clipped way of speaking, as if he thought words were not to be trifled with. The face, with channels cleaving the sides of his thin mouth, looked as uncompromising as granite, an impression heightened by the direct blue eyes. Bawtry had begun by neither liking nor disliking him, but association on several cases had given him a mounting respect. Not an easy man to cross, but a good man to have on your side, Bawtry judged.

Brooker said tersely: 'Sam will explain.' It was one of the nicer things about Brooker that he never tried to hog the limelight.

Bawtry went through it methodically, just the facts the way they had arranged themselves. At the end of it there was a small silence, as if they were waiting for Ballinger.

In fact, it was Ted Fallon who spoke first, after making a dry sound like a chuckle. 'A Ned on a bike — well, that's new, anyway.' He took out his scarred pipe and started ramming shag tobacco in the bowl.

Brooker, characteristically sitting with his hands dangling between his knees, grinned. 'If Ted's going to smoke that bloody awful stuff again I'll have to light a cigar.'

'Yes.' Braxted, who rarely smoked, looked across at Bawtry. 'I'll borrow a cigarette — in self-defence.'

Bawtry slid a new packet of twenty Players across the wide desk. Ballinger said tentatively: 'I sense that you think these raids are the work of more than one man, perhaps a gang?'

'I'm not suggesting it as a proven certainty, but I think it's a tenable supposition, sir. In each incident a man of widely differing appearance has been involved.'

'Five banks robbed in as many days. It's too much. It also reads like a very carefully planned sequence.' Ballinger straightened his already impeccably positioned regimental tie. 'I understand that negative inquiries have been made among all known criminals in the metropolitan area.'

Bawtry nodded. 'Yes, so far as can be ascertained they're all clean.' His mouth twitched faintly. 'Mind you, these fellas always have alibis of one kind or another — but it's fair to say that this time the alibis seem to stand up.'

Fallon's overlong features, which often seemed to resemble those of a slightly saddened horse, lightened in a fleeting grin. 'Perhaps we should be looking at it from another angle.'

Ballinger's head jerked round. 'Go on, Fallon,' he said gently.

'New fellas moving into Liverpool.' He glanced at Brooker and Bawtry. 'I'd say at a guess that you've already thought of that.'

'The idea has occurred, yes.'

'You didn't stress it in your summary, Bawtry.' The Assistant Chief Constable sounded a little testy.

'I was keeping strictly to the established facts, sir. I thought you'd prefer it.'

'Yes, in reporting the actual circum-stances. Facts come first and rightly, but that doesn't mean we don't want to hear any theory you may have.'

'The only theory I have is the one Ted has just aired. I think we ought to follow it up.'

'How?'

'Widespread inquiries among all the local villains . . . '

Ballinger interrupted. 'I was under the impression that they'd already been seen.'

'They've been asked to account for their movements on the days in question, sir. Just that. But they haven't been asked if they know or have heard on the grapevine if there are any new faces around.'

Brooker said: 'I'll issue a new directive to all C.I.D. officers.'

'We could also get the Crime Squad to go through all known haunts with a fine toothcomb — the clubs these fellas hang out in. There's a chance somebody will have heard something.'

As he spoke Bawtry reflected, not for the first time, that being one of the Crime Squad mob would be tailor-made for him. In the C.I.D. you investigated reported crimes, big and little, any kind of crime. The Crime Squad roamed the city, in and out of smoke-filled clubs jammed with villains and Merseyside whores, constantly on the lookout for crimes before they were even committed, often working lunatic hours but without the disciplinary bull. Bawtry knew the work would suit him but he also knew that neither the Chief Con nor Ballinger would agree to a transfer because of his reputation in the C.I.D., notably as an interrogator.

There was another reason: being in the Crime Squad would erode still further the time he had with Carol, the beautiful copper-haired girl he had married the morning after they first went to bed together on the night he solved the murder of her sister. Carol was fourteen years younger and the age disparity sometimes troubled him, but she would have none of it. 'You've no notion what a terribly handsome man you are, Samuel Dennistoun Bawtry,' she had said more than once. And this was true.

Though he had a certain vanity about grooming — 'The best-dressed cop on the strength,' his subordinates called him — he had none about his attraction to women.

Ballinger said: 'I'll have the Crime Squad briefed, but that doesn't mean you won't also be needed. Looking back, I seem to recall that you have what can best be described as certain contacts?'

'Sam has some,' said Brooker. 'Suggest he chats them up. Another thing — if there are any new faces the local villains won't like it.'

Fallon set fire to his pipe, picking up a blotter to hit a few sparks dancing in the pungent fumes. 'Including today's incident, the total amount stolen in the five raids runs out at a little over £43,000. Not perhaps a stupendous sum.'

'Helluva sight more than any of us get for a year's hard graft.' This from Brooker, poker-faced. 'I take the point, though. They might've got forty-three thousand in a single raid on a big bank — but they might also have got caught. So they pick small branch banks with small staffs . . . better chance of getting away with it. In fact, they have — so far.'

Braxted mashed his unfinished cigarette out with an air of distaste. 'They might strike again. There's still plenty of small bank branches. We can't watch them all round the clock. On the other hand we could have them under surveillance at nine-thirty in the mornings — that seems to be the relevant time.'

'Do it,' said Ballinger. He stood up abruptly. 'We'll meet again tomorrow — same time, gentlemen. I hope you'll all have something to report.'

Bawtry and Brooker walked back into the C.I.D. room.

'*He hopes*,' said Brooker drily. 'I wouldn't care to bet on it just yet. We're up against some smart operators over this lot.'

'We'll probably put the arm on them in the end. We usually do.'

'We don't win, 'em all, Sam. There's enough unsolved crimes on the file.'

'You always get some. The detection

rate is high, just the same. Well, I'd better get moving.'

'Big Dave McTaggart would've been a good starting point, only he's on his holidays, doing fifteen months in Walton.' Brooker grinned. 'Not that he'd be pleased to see you, as you put him down.'

'I still might pay him a visit — fellas get to hear things in stir. But I'll try somewhere else first. See you.'

3

Bawtry walked to where he was going — an alley off Tithebarn Street, near what used to be Exchange Station. Down at the bottom was a small pub, a hideous architectural survival from the late Victorian era which hadn't yet fallen to the demolition squads re-carving the face of the city. He had been there before when looking for Smiler Dobie and Dobie was there now all right, the way he always was within minutes of opening time, sitting at a corner table with Ches Blake.

Others were there, too, including at least half a dozen men whose names and fingerprints were on the police records. Bawtry stood for a moment under the drifting pall of cigarette smoke, noting them. He was aware that they had also noted his presence, uneasily, though this time they didn't make the tactical mistake of flitting, like anonymous shadows, out of the side exit.

If Smiler Dobie was aware that a jack had walked in he wasn't showing it. In fact, he was aware of it because Ches Blake had leaned across the table to impart the information. But Smiler didn't turn immediately. He waited until Bawtry let a hand drop on his shoulder

Then he moved his roly-poly figure, not hurriedly. 'Morning, Mr. B.'

'And a very good morning to you, Smiler. You, too, Ches. I hope I find you both in your usual exuberant health.'

Ches Blake got a travestied grin out and hung it on his foxy face. Smiler Dobie justified his nickname by producing what could pass for a genuine one. Smiler was widely believed, when on form, to be able to con a bird off a tree and a blandly affable smile was an integral part of his public image. He considered Bawtry's observation as if submitting it to a test.

'We're great, Mr. B.,' he said at length.

'As if the jack cared,' sneered Ches.

'I'm sure we have his best wishes.'

Smiler reached out a pudgy hand for his pint of black-and-tan. 'You care to join us in one, Mr. B.?'

'I'll have a half of bitter with you lads.'

'Why not?' Smiler called out to one of the two barmaids, a buxom woman with a piled hair-do like an orange-coloured bird's nest. 'Always nice to have a drink with a member of the C.I.D.'

Bawtry took a seat. 'Well, that's fine, then. How's business?'

'We're doing all right,' said Smiler indifferently.

'Still working at the old scrap metal lark, eh.?'

'Enough to keep our heads above water.'

'And a trifle to spare, I don't doubt.' Dealing in scrap metal was Smiler's legitimate business. Every now and then it was also a front for business which was less than legitimate. Although far from being in the top flight of confidence tricksters, Smiler did well enough in a small way.

But Bawtry said nothing of this.

Instead, he merely remarked: 'See you're wearing another new whistle and flute.'

Smiler smoothed down the wide lapels of his pale grey herringbone suit. 'Got it yest'day from Hymie Lesser.'

'A good tailor,' said Bawtry approvingly. 'Made to measure, I take it?'

Dobie spread trunk-like arms. 'Is there some other way?'

'Not for the well-dressed man.' Bawtry grinned. 'As a matter of interest, we share the same tailor.'

'You always were better turned-out than the other cops, Mr. B. Some of your fellas go around in suits I wouldn't be fished out of the Mersey in.'

'Mind you, it runs into money — but worth it, eh?'

'Yeh, it's always worth it.' Smiler sank the rest of his black-and-tan and reached for the new one. 'Well, what's it all about, then?'

Bawtry recognised that the preliminary kidology, required by unwritten protocol, was over. He said directly: 'Another bank hold-up this morning, down near the waterfront. Makes five in as many days.

The Chief Con doesn't like it.'

The roly-poly man lit a cigarette and blew smoke at the match flame until it died. 'What's it got to do with us?' he asked softly.

'Nothing, I hope.'

'You can get stuffed, then.' This from Ches, bitterly.

Bawtry said amiably: 'This fella you pal out with, Smiler — he always takes a poor view of it when I drop in for a chat.'

Ches showed his teeth in something that was less than a smile. 'Happen it's because I know you lot, always on the lookout for a pinch.'

'I haven't accused you two of any specific tort or malfeasance,' said Bawtry equably.

'Talk English, can't you?'

'Putting it another way, I'm not feeling your collar or even trying to, Ches.'

'So what d'yer want with us, then?'

'It occurs to me that you might know something.'

'Who, me?'

'You're running true to form with that old 'Who, me?' routine.'

'You can get . . . '

'So you've already said. Bit difficult, that, though.'

'Funny, aren't we?'

Smiler raised a hand. It was the signal for Ches Blake to die temporarily, greatly respected. 'Robbing banks ain't up our street, Mr. B. — as you well know.'

'If I thought otherwise we'd be having this conversation — which I, for one, am enjoying — in a different place, Smiler.' Bawtry leaned forward. 'We're going on the theory that the hold-ups are the work of a gang — and foreigners, at that. Not a Merseyside mob, I mean.'

'Ah!' said Dobie.

'And I'm just wondering if you fellas or any of your mates might have heard on the grapevine about new-comers moving into the Pool.'

Smiler's schooled face betrayed nothing of whatever thoughts he was having. He said carelessly: 'What makes you think we might've heard something?'

'You hear things, don't you? Just that.'

'Yeh, now and then. So do the Crime Squad mob — why don't you ask them?'

'We're doing that, Smiler. In the meantime I'm asking you straight out: have you seen any new faces in the bailiwick?'

'If you want a straight answer I can give it you — no!'

'We think the fella who did the bank job this morning may have got away on a pedal bike and . . . ' Bawtry stopped. A sudden look had come on the other's face. 'Thought of something, Smiler?'

'I might have.' Dobie grinned. 'How much are you paying, Mr. B.?'

'Depends what the information's worth. There is, of course, the point that a citizen's duty is to aid the law without expectation of financial gain.'

'It ought to be worth summat, just the same.'

'I'll judge that when I know what it is.'

Smiler manufactured a sigh. 'All right, then. It was like this — I was up in the Liverpool 8 district earlier in the day and seen a fella leave a bike outside one of them big old houses they have up there. I thought it was funny. I mean him walking off and leaving it to be pinched by the kids round there.'

'Describe him.'

'Thirty-five or so. Lightish hair, thick on his neck. Well-dressed. He had tinted specs on, gold-rimmed specs. That fit?'

'It fits. He just propped the bike against the front of a house and left it?'

'That's right. I thought it was funny, like I told you. I mean if you leave a bike or anything else lying about up there it just bloody well vanishes, in quick-sticks.'

'What makes you think it might've have had something to do with a bank robbery?'

'I didn't think it had, I didn't connect it with no hold-up until you said the fella might have got away on a bike and then I remembered.' Smiler grinned again. 'A bike would be a good way of getting clear, come to think of it. And the description tallies, eh?'

'Yes. A man who looked like this character you saw held up the bank this morning, a small branch bank in Lexton Street.'

'How about the other hold-ups what've already been in the papers?'

'Not the same fella. In fact, they all looked different.'

'You reckon it's a gang?'

'It's possible. You don't happen to have had a tip-off that a new mob are operating here, or do you?'

Ches Blake fished a cigarette dimp out of his jacket pocket and set fire to it. Smiler Dobie sat very still, as if trying to make his mind up about something. Finally, he said: 'There's a rumour — and it's not more than a rumour — about some Manchester fellas being in Liverpool.'

'What fellas?'

'Don't know. Like I said, it's just a rumour.'

'Details?'

'There aren't any. It's just a whisper that a Manchester mob may have moved in. Nowt more definite than that. If there was I'd tell you.'

'Because you and your mates don't want foreigners muscling in?'

'We don't welcome outsiders, you

know that. Not as it'd make any difference to me and Ches personally if they stuck up a dozen banks. It's not our line, as you well know.'

'There are some around who've been known to rob a bank. Like Nick Lanigan and Joe Wilkes — only they've left the district, last heard of down in the Smoke.'

'So I've heard.' Dobie's mouth creased faintly. 'I also heard they got no big welcome down there,'

Bawtry drank some of his bitter slowly. Then he said: 'This fella who ditched the bike — where'd he go? Which direction?'

'He set off like he might be going towards the old Central Station.'

'You watched him?'

'Not to make a business of it. I just happened to see him going that way.'

'You were interested enough to look, weren't you?'

'Yeh — because of him leaving his bike in a place like that. Anything you haven't nailed down just disappears up there.'

'It could be our man.' Bawtry grinned. 'Pity you didn't follow him.'

'Give over. I didn't have no reason. I was up there collecting scrap metal, or trying to.'

'You and Ches here?'

'No, Ches wasn't with me. Like I say, it struck me as odd this fella leaving his bike, but I didn't think much to it until you came asking.' Smiler put his tankard down. 'Any road, I've told you *summat*, Mr. B. What's it worth.'

'About a quid, I'd say.'

'What, with inflation and everything!'

Silently, Bawtry passed a five pound note across. 'If you hear of anything else, especially anything that could lead to an identification, there might be more.'

Smiler trousered the note. 'We'll keep our eyes and ears open, Mr. B. One thing none of us here wants is a parcel of Manchester types trespassing in the Pool. You like another drink?'

'Not now, thanks all the same.'

'Don't thank me — I'd be using police money.' Smiler chuckled fatly. 'It'll all go on wallop.'

'A disturbing thought. Well, thanks for the information, such as it is.'

36

'It might lead to summat, you never can tell.'

'We'll see.'

'From small beginnings . . . '

'Or a journey of a thousand miles begins with a single step, as the Chinese say around Pitt Street.' Bawtry stood up, dropping powerful hands on their shoulders. 'Take care, lads.'

'We always take care, Mr. B.,' said Dobie amiably.

Bawtry walked to Central Station. It was no longer in use as the main line terminus on the Manchester run. So why should a Manchester villain — if that was what the man with the bicycle was — go there? A thought stirred far down in Bawtry's mind. By the time he got there it was on the surface.

The questioning took a little time before someone on the station staff remembered seeing a blond man go into a lavatory and, better still, remembered seeing a different-looking man come out all of ten minutes later.

'Which cubicle?'

'I'll show you, Mr. Bawtry.'

Bawtry went in and stared round. Why should anyone spend ten or more minutes in a public lavatory? He grinned at the thought and the obvious answer. Just the same, he went on looking. Finally, he reached down behind the lavatory bowl and picked up a strand of what looked like ash blond hair. He put it in an envelope and went back to Headquarters.

A quarter of an hour later he was in possession of the interesting information that the hair almost certainly belonged to a wig.

4

Julian Charles Arbor let himself into the small flat he had taken near St. John's Precinct and double-locked the door behind him. Then he walked into the fitted kitchen and drew the curtains, not solely because it was a brilliantly sunny day. He tipped the soft leather sack on to the breakfast table and methodically counted the money. It was £7,567 — which made the total for the five robberies £43,601.

'Better than ten years' slog in rep. old boy . . . ' The spoken words were like music in his ears.

The relevant thing was that Julian Arbor was an actor. He was also a good one and would probably have done better than his words suggested because sooner or later he would have made the breakthrough. But more than half a decade in repertory, even though he had got out of the really small time and into a major city, had begun to chafe. You had to be word-perfect on the play you were currently appearing in while learning another and taking a preliminary reading of the one you were going to have to do in a fortnight's time. Not that learning a script came hard to him. He had the photographic mind and total recall which is God's gift to an actor. Some didn't have it or had it only partially and blew-up in their lines and had to improvise, hoping their colleagues would cue them back in. Julian could completely memorise a full script in an hour and a half, usually doing it lying in bed. He could memorise the entire play, all the other parts as well as his own. It was a knack; either you had it or you didn't have it. Apart from that, he had a fine voice, flexible and adaptable to whatever character he was playing.

He knew he was lucky to be able to do all this with ease, but he told himself that the knowledge was small compensation for the demands of rep and the travelling on wet Sundays to the next town and playing in half-empty theatres, those which had survived the impact of television. True, he had had parts in one-off TV plays, but so far he hadn't made it into a thirteen-week series — a goal for most actors. The only steadily-recurring work he got outside repertory was on radio as a voice impersonator. This was because he could produce almost any kind of accent at will, from Manchester to Memphis and back via Hong-Kong.

It was this, plus something he read in the newspapers about the vulnerability of small branch banks, which had triggered the idea that was to kite his personal wealth into the £40,000 bracket in a single week, no tax.

He was still in London at the time, resting — an actor's euphemism for being out of a job. He had just done four weeks at a small theatre in the East End, an experimental art theatre which only stayed in business because it was subsidised by a grant from public funds. Now he had three weeks out before his next engagement, which would take him to a newly-opened repertory theatre up in Yorkshire. Just a single week with a touring outfit putting on *avant-garde* stuff by earnest young writers to whom the notion of a play having a beginning, a middle and an end was anathema. In fact, their kind of play was anathema to Julian Arbor who, although still in his mid-thirties, liked what was patronisingly known as the well-made play; the only really happy time he had had as an actor in the last two years was appearing in *Loyalties*.

Julian had £151 on current account, nothing on deposit and no investments, and lived in a bed-sitter at Earls Court, existing on pub lunches of sausage and chips as the main meal of the day; a poor substitute for a slap-up dinner in a favourite Soho *ristorante* with a pretty girl. Girls? He liked them, but he hadn't been with one in months, even on a platonic basis. This wasn't because he didn't meet any — but, quite simply, because he couldn't afford to invite one out, with work coming his way only intermittently. In fact, the only booking on the horizon was the coming week in Yorkshire and that only deputising for a member of the company who had caught the flu.

Then, out of the blue, he got the chance of a full season's work at a new repertory theatre up in Liverpool. He was in the pub where he ate when Gerry Cromack came in. Cromack was a thickset man in his late forties, an expatriate American from New York, though he was born in Dallas, Texas.

'Thought I might find you here, Julian,' he said. 'How's everything?'

'You ought to know, you're my agent. But in case you're in any doubt, the operative word is lousy.'

'No, it isn't,' said Cromack amiably.

'You mean that week in Yorkshire?'

'No, I don't. You can forget that. Something better has come up.'

'Oh, what?'

'A season's work. The money isn't enormous, but it's better than you've been seeing lately.'

'Where?'

'A new rep theatre in Liverpool, the Riverside Theatre. Charles Leeming, the director, wants a new leading

43

man — the one he had in mind
has cried off, going to Canada on a
tour. Leeming came on the phone this
morning and asked if I could recommend
someone. I recommended you.'

'Well, a lot of thanks, Gerry. A season
— how long?'

'Thirty-six weeks residence. The job's
yours, if you want it.'

'I'm going to buy you a large Scotch,'
said Julian.

'A small one. Don't get carried away.'

'How much are they paying?'

Cromack told him. Julian said: 'You're
right about the money not being enormous,
but on the other hand it's not bad. I'll
take it.'

'I thought you would, that's why I
came here. Knew I'd find you eating
your frugal lunch at around this time.'

'Frugal is about it. No, actually,
sausage and chips are all right — but
not every bloody day in the week.'
Julian ordered two small Bells and said
tentatively: 'What sort of plays?'

'Revivals, mostly. Maugham, Rattigan,
Lonsdale — all the writers you most

admire. You'll have a ball.'

'Yes, I will. And thanks again, Gerry.'

'Happy to oblige. Besides, you're exactly right for the job. I gave you a big build-up. Know you won't let me down. Among other things, they're doing a play with an American character and they want the accent to be right. Not the traditional Englishman's idea of how Americans talk. That's up your street, too.'

'American — which State?'

'Mine. Say something Texan.'

Julian picked up the morning newspaper he had brought with him and read aloud at random.

Cromack grinned. 'Swell — it would deceive my dear old Aunt Harriet . . . ' He broke off. 'What's the matter?'

'Nothing, I was just thinking.' Julian looked again at what he had just read: *Bank employees are worried by the mounting wave of armed hold-ups, particularly on branch banks which are considered to be increasingly at risk because of their small staff . . .* There was more in the same vein.

45

'Thinking what?' Cromack asked.

Julian laughed. 'It was what I just read out for you — it' struck me that an actor who can change his appearance and voice at will might do better raiding a bank.'

'Until they put him behind bars, yeah.'

Julian re-folded the newspaper and put it back on the bar. 'I'd better settle for this job you've fixed. When do I start?'

'Three weeks from today.'

'I'm booked to go to this godforsaken place in Yorkshire then.'

'I've already got you out of that, Julian.'

'You appear to have arranged everything.'

'But naturally — I'm your agent and it was too good a chance to pass up. The small rep going to Yorkshire say they'll take Robert Bronton instead.' Cromack drank the rest of his whisky and bought two more. 'Before I forget — Leeming says there's a small bachelor flat available right in the city centre. Furnished. The guy who's going to Canada was to have had it. Now it's yours for the season.'

'Sounds all right. I hope the rent is.'

'I understand it's reasonable, the way

things are.' Cromack looked at his gold wrist watch. 'Leeming would like to see you this afternoon. Two-thirty at his office in Bloomsbury, you know where it is?'

'Yes.'

'I must be off. Have a swell time up in Liverpool and let me know how you make out.'

'I won't forget,' said Julian. He stayed on in the pub for another twenty minutes, savouring the agreeable thought of steady work in the sort of plays he liked. It was some time later when the other thought re-surfaced in his mind. He grinned at the recollection of what he had said to Gerry Cromack: just a barmy idea out of the blue, the kind of throwaway line you dreamed-up in a pub talk.

That night he bought himself a slap-up dinner in Soho, washed down with a bottle of Chianti. He took a taxi back to Earls Court and when he went to bed he couldn't sleep for a while because the idea was still moving in his mind. When he woke up next morning it was still there.

★ ★ ★

47

In the fortnight before he had to go up to Liverpool to rehearse it continued to grow. At first he tried to dismiss it; then, by degrees, he started to take it seriously. With time on his hands, and at no risk because at this stage he wasn't going to do anything illegal, he decided to put it to the test.

On a clear day in late April he walked into the same pub with a subtly changed facial appearance and wavy brown hair on top of his own and denim casuals he had bought for the purpose. He was posing as an American. If he could get away with it face to face with Syd Fenner, who owned the place, he could get away with anything.

He walked up to the bar and said, in a slight drawl: 'Whisky sour, bartender.'

Fenner, a wiry man with a bony head packed with experience, said: 'Whisky sour coming up.' He slid the drink across the counter, looking at Julian directly for a moment. Julian's mouth went dry, but Fenner's next words dispelled the sudden sense of alarm.

'Over here on a visit, sir?'

'Yeah, three – four weeks.' Julian put a five pound note on the bar. Fenner rang up the price and gave him the change.

'Have one yourself,' said Julian.

'Thanks, sir.'

'You're welcome.' Julian glanced down the bar. There were three men who knew him both by sight and name.

Fenner served another customer, came back and said: 'This your first trip to England?'

'I guess so. My folks came from England and I've always promised myself a visit.'

'You'll be going to Stratford-on-Avon, places like that, eh?'

'A week in London, then a tour — want to see as much as I can pack into the time.'

The pub started to fill with a sudden rush of customers. Fenner said: 'You'll have to excuse me, sir. See you again, perhaps?'

'Sure will.' Julian finished his drink and strolled down the bar. One of the three men saw him, but gave no sign of recognition.

Julian walked out. He was conscious of the slightly heady sensation which comes to a man who has taken a long chance and seen it come off. Better test it again, though.

In the next week he tested it six more times in widely differing circumstances, using a new identity on each occasion and deliberately facing people who knew what Julian Arbor looked like. They didn't know him, and by the time he was due to go to Liverpool the idea had become an obsession.

5

There was a time when the rich merchants of Liverpool lived in noble Georgian houses on wide sweeping streets in the heart of the city and bought black slaves shipped into the port from the west coast of Africa. The merchants and the slaves are long gone. The Georgian houses are still there, but they are no longer noble, despite the elegant staircases and the decorative entrances. They stand, flaking and forlorn, mute witnesses to what decades of neglect have done — and, by an ironic twist of fate, the people who live in them now are the descendants of the slaves who once served their rich masters.

The city itself, bulldozed and partially re-faced, still has derelict warehouses, boarded-up shops and abandoned docks with a residue of inner slums flowing like a shabby tide almost to the walls of the two great cathedrals, Anglican and Roman Catholic. The massive urban clearance drive, launched in the optimistic flush of the Sixties, now looks like a series of self-inflicted wounds — with thousands of inner city residents uprooted and dropped down in overspill new towns like Skelmersdale and Runcorn. With them went the small businesses, the light industries — and the rating revenue. The great port itself has declined, its economic base disappearing from under its feet by the industrial shift South.

The enterprising young have gone, or too many of them. And while Liverpool struggles to rise again from the effects of planning campaigns, hoping that one day the middle classes will be attracted back to a still proud city, there is now a high proportion of people who are old, unskilled, unable to cope, just plain poor — or black.

Five per cent of the population are black and most of them live in Liverpool 8 in the dilapidated Georgian houses crouched like faded aristocrats among the high-rise flats, small council houses and blackened terrace homes around Nile

Street, Tiber Street and Pilgrim Street. Not so long ago you could walk around Liverpool 8 without qualms. Today white people are not encouraged to go unaccompanied into this bleak and desolate jungle of scattered refuse, broken glass, endless graffiti, even half-wild dogs and cats.

Out of the crumbling Georgian homes come the black teenage boys made sullenly insolent by inability to get anything but the most menial work, often not even that, and the young coloured girls teetering on huge platform shoes, chewing gum and looking — for what? Too often men. Prostitution has always existed in Liverpool but now it has risen and is still rising.

Bawtry went there with George Lucas, a detective-sergeant. They walked because it isn't far from Police Headquarters, housed in what was once a blind asylum. An 'in' joke among the police holds that the place is still an asylum, but the humour is affectionate, not astringent.

'We'll be dead lucky if we find that bike, Sam,' Lucas mused. 'Like looking for the needle in the haystack.'

'It's worth a try, George.' Bawtry slackened his long stride slightly, though Lucas, who was less tall, was keeping up with him. 'We'll see if Millie Laya knows anything, for a start.'

Millicent Laya worked in the district as a community relations officer. A forty-year-old part West Indian on her father's side; the other part Welsh. Millie Laya's skin was several shades lighter than most of those she tried to help, many of whom spent money they could ill-afford on hair-straighteners and skin-lighteners. Bawtry remembered Millie once telling him about finding a twelve-year-old girl scrubbing her skin with detergent powder in the hope of getting it to go pale, like a white girl's.

The office was up near Myrtle Street and Millie was in, seated at a desk wrestling with paper work.

'Hello Millie,' said Bawtry.

She made a quick smile. 'Good morning, Mr. B., what brings you here?' The smile went away. 'Not trouble, is it?'

54

'Just an inquiry, Millie. A man held up a bank this morning — a white man. We think he got away on a bicycle. Shortly afterwards a man answering to his description was seen abandoning a bike in Liverpool 8 — not far from here, as a matter of fact.'

'Yes?' Millie said it hesitantly.

'Well, any bike left unattended round here would be a bit of a magnet, wouldn't you say?'

'Yes, I suppose it would . . . '

'We're not looking for a bicycle thief, Millie. Even if we find someone who took possession of the bike there won't be a prosecution.'

'Oh?' She sounded relieved. 'I'm glad. I wouldn't like to say anything that could cause trouble. Morale is very low here already, particularly among the second and third generation blacks.'

'I know.'

'The authorities work hard at integration but all the time segregation seems to get worse.' She sighed. 'Social workers, people like me, and all the authorities deny that there's prejudice against black people when all the time it's a fact of life.'

'And the appearance of a police officer in Liverpool 8 doesn't reassure — I know that, too.'

'Two police officers.' Miss Laya smiled at Lucas.

Bawtry said levelly: 'I have to ask — do you know if any boy or girl round here has come into possession of a bicycle?'

For a moment she seemed to hesitate again. 'You're not going to make a case of it, you say?'

'You have my word on it, Millie.'

'All right then. Young Ronnie Albertson called to me about an hour or so ago when I was out walking. He was riding a bike, an old one it was. I thought he must've borrowed it because I'm sure he wouldn't have the money to buy one, even if it was offered cheap.'

'It mightn't be the same machine, but we'd like to know for certain. Where can we find this boy?'

'I can give you his address, though he's more likely to be out with his mates. They tend to hang about Sylvester Square most mornings.' She scribbled the address on a piece of notepaper. 'One thing — don't bring me into it, Mr. Bawtry. It wouldn't help my work if it was known I'd talked to you.'

The address was near Nile Street, a *cul de sac* of rundown terrace houses aching for the demolition squad. Both Bawtry and Lucas knew it well enough, but they went first to the square. A group of boys, threequarters of them black, were there.

Bawtry called out: 'Which one of you is Ronnie Albertson?'

For a moment no one spoke. Then the tallest of them, a gangling boy with an Afro hair style, answered.

'Who wants him, then?'

'We'd just like to chat with him, that's all,' said Bawtry mildly.

The tall youth eyed them, up and down.

'Fuzz!' He spat the word.

Several of the others started to move, fanning out in different directions.

Bawtry said, loudly this time: 'We don't want to book him. We simply want a bit of information.'

The tall boy made an arm movement. The others stopped. 'We got nothing to tell you, copper.'

'You don't know yet what we want. What's your name?'

'Joey Kalmar — what's it to you?'

'I just like to know who I'm talking to. *Is* Ronnie Albertson here?'

'You weren't just saying it, about not going to book him?'

'We're not going to book him.'

'Awright.' He jerked his head sideways. A thin boy with crinkled hair and only light facial colouring said sullenly: 'I'm Ronnie Albertson. Whaddyer want?'

'A white man left a bicycle near here earlier today. Did you find it?'

'I might have . . . '

'It doesn't matter if you rode it away, it doesn't matter. But if you've got it we want to see it.' Bawtry moved closer. 'A bike was left near here by a man who had just robbed a bank.'

'I didn't rob no bank, mister . . . '

'I'm quite sure you didn't. But this man did and we need to examine the bike. Understand?'

Ronnie looked at Joey, who said: 'Better tell the fuzz where it is.'

'It's in the alley, just off the square — over there.' Ronnie nodded in the direction.

'Bring it out, son.'

'Awright, then.' Ronnie wheeled the bike out of the alley. 'I thought it was okay, with this fella ditching it, like.'

'You mean you thought it was all right to take an abandoned bike?'

'Yeh, that's what I thought.'

The others crowded round now. One of them said: 'Why would a fella what's robbed a bank use an old grid like this?'

'Nobody'd be looking for a bank robber on a bike,' said Joey. 'They always has cars.'

Bawtry said: 'Perhaps one of you'll ride it to Headquarters. You'd all better come — we'll need your fingerprints.'

'What for?' Joey's voice edged.

'His fingerprints may be on the bike. We'll need those of anyone else who touched it — so that we can count you out.'

They all looked at Joey Kalmar. He

59

shrugged and said: 'Okay, fellas.'

Ronnie wheeled the bike to Headquarters, with the rest tagging on behind. Half an hour later Bawtry had their dabs. They were the only ones.

George Lucas said: 'Chummy must've been wearing gloves.'

'They all wear them these days, they get the idea from watching television.' Bawtry lit a cigarette and went on: 'The machine was almost certainly bought from a secondhand dealer. You'd think he'd notice if the buyer was wearing gloves — unusual at this time of the year.'

'Happen he wasn't, but wiped everything off later and then put gloves on when he used the bike to go to the bank.'

'It's possible. But we'll need to check with the dealers. We have a list of them. Get several d-cs to see them, George.'

It was afternoon when the reports came in. Forty used bicycles sold in the last week. Only one of the dealers remembered a customer with gloves.

'No progress,' said Lucas laconically.

'It's a start. Get on the blower to every

dealer in town with a request to keep the next customer waiting on any pretext while he calls us back.'

'I'll do it right away.' Lucas put the list on a desk and started dialling.

A week passed. There were almost daily calls from dealers and detectives got out there in time to interview the customers. Every one was able to produce a genuine alibi for the five relevant times.

And there were no more bank raids. Not yet.

6

Julian was ready to quit the theatre company. With more than forty thousand pounds, mostly in used notes, he no longer needed to work. But an ingrained caution suggested that he should stay on. The fact that a member of the company had resigned was not necessarily a suspicious circumstance, but there was always the chance that the police might get to hear of it and start wondering. A long chance, perhaps so long that it could be discounted out of hand. Better not take it, though. For the time being at least.

There was another and more pressing reason. He had started an affair with Lynne Mayes and if he suddenly slung his hook without so much as leaving an address she would think he had another girl and start talking — and it was less than a long chance that the situation could be potentially dangerous.

They had met by chance in a restaurant off Church Street one night after the show. The place was almost full. The head waiter drifted up carrying a sheaf of jumbo-sized menus.

'Table for one, sir?'

'If you can manage it.'

'We only have three vacant seats — I'm afraid you'll have to share a table, sir.'

Julian, whose eyes were ranging the room, said: 'I'll take the one on the right — if the young lady there doesn't object.'

'I'll inquire for you.' The head waiter went away. He was back in moments. 'No objection, sir.' He weaved through the diners.

Julian bowed. 'Awfully good of you to let me share your table.'

'That's all right.'

He slid into the vacant seat, regarding her unobtrusively, noting the smooth rounded face framed by a mass of dark brown hair and the figure which announced itself through the blue-and-white polka dot dress. In her late twenties, he judged. No rings on the significant finger on her left hand.

'I'd better introduce myself,' he said. 'My name's Arbor — Julian Arbor.'

Her long mouth smiled. 'I know you, Mr. Arbor.'

He stared.

'Putting it more accurately, I've seen you before. And I know your name.'

'Ah, I understand — you've seen me in the theatre?'

'That's right. I was there tonight.' She put a slim hand across the table. 'I'm Lynne Mayes and it's a pleasure to make your acquaintance, Mr. Arbor.'

He took the proffered hand, holding it a few seconds longer than was strictly necessary. 'I hope you weren't disappointed. With the show, I mean.'

'On the contrary, I thought it was fine. As a matter of fact, I go there every week.'

'Alone?'

'Sometimes with a girl friend, but mostly by myself.'

'Really?'

'You sound surprised.'

'I am, a little. I wouldn't have thought

you'd lack an escort, if I may be permitted the observation.'

She laughed. 'You've made it, anyway. Answering your observation, perhaps I'm fussy about who I go out to dinner with.'

'Then I must take it as a compliment that you didn't object to my sharing your table.'

'Perhaps. On the other hand, there's a shortage of seats.'

'Not so complimentary, after all, I fear.'

'Except that if I hadn't liked you in the theatre you wouldn't be sitting here.'

'That's better — though the man you saw on stage wasn't the real me, you know.'

'Meaning you were just playing a part, being a different person every week. I realise that. Incidentally, you do it very well.'

'Thank you.' A floor waiter came up. Julian ordered prawn cocktail, minestrone and roast Norfolk duckling. 'You haven't any wine.'

'I was trying to make my mind up

about that . . . you choose.'

He picked up the wine list. 'White or red?'

'White, I think.'

'The medium-dry Bordeaux, Villa Cliqot, is usually very good. A litre, eh?'

'No, just a bottle will do. I don't drink much.'

'As you wish.'

The waiter said: 'I'll send the wine steward, sir.'

There was a slight pause. The girl ended it. 'Have you always been an actor, Mr. Arbor?'

'What makes you ask?'

'You don't look like an actor.'

Julian grinned. 'I'm not quite sure how to take that. But — how should an actor look?'

'I imagined they looked . . . well, a bit stagey, even away from the theatre.'

'And I don't?'

'Not really.'

'I'm glad to hear it. I don't care for the kind of pro who goes around advertising his calling. Few of us do, as a matter of fact. Not these days. However, the answer to your question is yes, I've always been an actor, apart from about seven months working on a newspaper when I left university.'

'Journalism, you mean?'

'Yes. I decided that I wasn't going to be much good at it and the theatre had always attracted me. I hadn't much money but enough to enrol in drama school, after which I was lucky enough to get work with a touring company. They didn't pay very well, but I learned the business.'

'And never looked back?'

'Frequently — acting is an overcrowded profession and very chancy, especially for a man. However, I suppose I can't complain.'

'I don't know a great deal about the theatre — but I'd have thought the company you're with is a good one.'

'It has a pretty good rating, but it's still not the peak of ambition.'

'Are you ambitious?'

'Very.'

The wine waiter came. Julian poured

the wine and said: 'How about yourself — what do you do?'

'I'm a buyer for one of the big stores.'

'Do you like it?'

'Very much. I've only had the job just over a year, starting as a sales assistant. Then this post became vacant and I got it.'

'You must have been well thought of — it's a pretty responsible job, isn't it?'

'Well, yes, it is. You have to know what to buy, what the customers want or are likely to want. So far I haven't boobed, said she, keeping fingers crossed.'

'It involves quite a bit of travelling, doesn't it?'

'Some of the time, yes. As a matter of fact, I'm going to Paris later this month and then on to Rome. We're interested in some of the new Italian styles, particularly for the younger women.'

'They're the big spenders these days, aren't they?'

'They tend to spend a fair amount on clothes — fortunately for persons like me.'

'You come from Liverpool?'

'No, my parents live in Southport. I went to grammar school there and started in one of the shops on Lord Street before I came to Liverpool.'

'You live in the city?'

'At first I had a bedsitter, but after I got this job I moved closer to the store. I've quite a nice flat, small but modern and nice, in Dorchester Close . . . ' She broke off. 'Have I said something?'

Julian laughed. 'It's the coincidence — that's where I'm living. Number 4a Dorchester Close.'

'Well, that certainly is a coincidence. My place is 9b, one floor up from yours. Funny we haven't met before.'

'Just missed each other, I suppose. We can walk home together — unless you've come in a car.'

'I have a car, but I didn't bother to use it — the theatre's within walking distance, and you can keep to the main streets.'

'Just as well, these days. Get off the well-lit thoroughfares and you run the risk of being mugged — or worse, if you're a girl.'

'Yes, I know. There's quite a lot of

violence going on.'

'Too much. You won't mind if we walk home together?'

'Why should I?' she said innocently.

Julian chuckled. 'There used to be a time when actors were classed as no better than rogues and vagabonds.'

'I'm sure you don't fit that description, Mr. Arbor.'

'I hope not!' Rogue fitted, though, didn't it? But forty grand lifted him clean out of the vagabond class. The thoughts were running through his head as he went on: 'If we're going to be friends — and I hope we are — you can call me Julian.'

'All right — Julian.'

'That sounds better, Lynne.'

They finished the meal and sat on for a while over coffee and brandy. The head waiter drifted up.

Julian said: 'I'll pick up the bill.'

'No, really, I'd rather pay my share.'

'Please allow me.'

'I'd prefer . . . '

'I'm going to insist. If you feel strongly about it, you can pay next time.'

'There's going to be a next time, then?'

She eyed him quizzically.

'More than one, I hope, Lynne.'

He paid the bill and they walked home together.

Julian said: 'Can I invite you in for a final drink?'

'You've already done it, haven't you?'

'I suppose I have. And?'

She hesitated, but for no more than a moment. 'I'll come in.'

He made two drinks and switched the colour TV on. They sat together on the settee watching the late newscast.

'There's an old movie on after this,' Julian said. 'Do you want to see it?'

'I don't think so.' She put her drink on the coffee table. 'I really ought to be going . . . '

He stood up, switched the set off and came back, not speaking.

'Penny for them,' she said, smiling.

'If you must know, I'm fighting a losing battle with an overmastering desire to kiss you.'

She half-turned, looking at him enigmatically. He cradled an arm round her shoulders. She came towards him

71

unresistingly. He went down to her in a long kiss.

'You're beautiful, Lynne.' His free hand began moving.

'I didn't say you could do that,' she said faintly.

He didn't answer. She laid back with her eyes almost closed.

A little while later they were in his bed.

* * *

The first bank job was the hardest — not in its execution but in the tension it imposed on him. He had planned it in meticulous detail, every move thought out and mentally rehearsed over and over again; but there was always the possibility of the unforeseen thing, the chance of something going utterly wrong, the small thing you couldn't anticipate.

It was a branch bank off Smithdown Road near Toxteth Park Cemetery. The proximity fired the sombre thought: 'Hope it's not going to be my graveyard!' It wasn't, but as he approached the point

72

of no return he had to fight off a panic desire to turn and flee while there was still time. His nerves felt taut, like stretched piano wires. Then he was through the front door and going up to the counter and the panic left him, the way first night nerves leave an actor the moment he walks to centre stage. He could remember a score of occasions when he had stood in the wings with sweating palms waiting for his cue and once he had been given it he went out there, hands suddenly dry, his voice and movements under control. It was something like that when he got to the bank counter. He could hear himself speaking the carefully memorised lines, see himself making the rehearsed movements, like in a play; in some odd way he had the illusion of standing outside himself as if he were his own audience.

Then it was over, in minutes it was over, and he was outside the bank riding the first of the second-hand bicycles he was to buy and abandon. He turned right into Tunnel Road and left the bike where he had planned — at the back of Edge

Hill station. There were people about but nobody was looking at him, he was sure of it. He went into a lavatory, removed the wig and facial make-up, reversed the raincoat he had bought for the purpose and put it back on — over the soft leather sack slung on slim straps round his neck. He walked down a maze of small streets to Brownlow Hill. A taxi loomed, with its *For Hire* sign illuminated, but he let it pass. Taxi drivers remembered things. True, his appearance now bore no resemblance to that of the man who had held up the bank. Better to walk, though; not hurriedly. He crossed Lime Street into Ranelagh Street, turned right and in a few more moments was safe in his flat, up-ending the sack on the bed with shaking hands. The notes scattered over the quilted overlay. He re-assembled them in piles, counting: £4,375 for five or six minutes' work. Except that you had to add the time spent in thinking and planning and rehearsing. Well, all right, it was still a fat rate of profit, wasn't it?

Julian could hear himself breathing in jerks. He looked at his hands, spreading them. They were still shaking a little. He wadded the money into a suitcase, locked it and put it on the floor of the fitted wardrobe and locked that as well. Then he went into the lounge and poured himself a powerful Scotch. He wasn't addicted to drink, but now he needed one. He had two, the first one straight and straight down. He added water to the second and drank it more slowly. It was the first time in his life that he had ever taken a drink at ten-thirty in the morning. He stripped off his clothes, got into pyjamas and went back to bed.

It was nearly two in the afternoon when he awoke. No hangover, he hadn't drunk enough for a hangover. He looked at his spread hands again. No more shaking. He stood under the shower, changed into casuals and went out to lunch. By half-past three he was back in the flat. He felt restless, disinclined to read, though he was fond of reading. At four o'clock the telephone rang. He almost literally jumped. He reached for the receiver.

'Yes?' He could only get the word out with difficulty.

'Is that Merseyside Radio and TV Services?'

'I'm afraid not . . . '

'I must have the wrong number then. Sorry.'

'That's all right.'

There was a distant click as the caller hung up. Julian let the receiver slide back on its rest, breathing relief. Thoughts moved in his mind. What the hell am I relieved about? If the police were after him they wouldn't ring up, they'd call, wouldn't they? Just the same, he felt a sensation of relief.

The phone didn't ring again and the police didn't call and when it was time to go down to the theatre he was feeling elated.

After the show Giles Lester, the director, said: 'You were in top form tonight, Julian.'

'Was I?'

'Best performance I've seen in a long time.'

'Thanks.'

'Like to join me in a drink?'

'The pubs will be shut.'

'I'm a member of the Press Club. You can come as my guest.'

'That means I won't be able to buy you one back.'

Lester grinned. 'It's your lucky day then.'

'Yes,' said Julian.

★ ★ ★

He made the other bank raids on consecutive mornings and didn't need to take a drink afterwards.

7

A week went by, a week of intensive investigation and the re-examination of witnesses; but still no lead.

Ballinger said: 'There must be a clue somewhere. Nobody can pull off five bank raids without leaving a clue — still less a number of men.'

'If there is a clue we haven't found it.' This from Brooker.

'That scarcely needs saying, Brooker. Suppose you run through everything you and your team have done.'

Brooker did it.

Ballinger said quietly: 'I can't fault you on that, but somewhere along the line we *must* have missed something. What do you think, Bawtry?'

'It doesn't necessarily follow, Sir.'

'You mean the raiders have completely covered their tracks?'

'So far, yes. If we keep at it happen we'll come up with something.'

'Meaning what?'

'They almost always make a mistake — if not at the time the crime is committed then later.'

'Time is something we're running out of, Bawtry. Every day that passes minimises the chances of making an arrest.'

Braxted said: 'A group of men . . . you'd think their presence would be known by some of the local villains.'

'Sam's seen some of the local Neds, two in particular,' said Fallon.

'Smiler.Dobie and Ches Blake,' said Brooker. 'They didn't know of any new faces in the patch.'

'Dobie saw a man leaving a bicycle against the side of a house in Liverpool 8, a man who could be a bank robber,' said Bawtry. 'But I have mentioned that.'

Ballinger nodded. 'You found strands of what could be a wig in the men's convenience at Central Station. Good work — but it still doesn't take us closer.'

'No, sir . . . ' Bawtry paused.

Ballinger let a small silence stay for a

few moments. Then: 'Are you thinking of something, Bawtry?'

'It's nothing factual, sir.'

'I didn't suggest that.' Ballinger's voice acquired a cutting edge. 'I asked if you were thinking of something.'

'I imagine all of us have thoughts in a situation like this, sir,'

'I'm asking you personally. Well?'

Bawtry felt irritated. He disliked being forced to disclose theories before he had checked them, but he saw that he now had no choice.

'I thought you preferred to have facts, sir.'

'Facts first, always — but thoughts about the known facts aren't excluded. If you have any I want to know what they are.'

'We've assumed that the bank robberies have been carried out by several men. Crimes of this nature often are. One man does the actual hold-up, another acts as lookout and another stays in the getaway car with the engine idling ready.'

'Go on, Bawtry.'

'Well, sir, we've also considered the

possibility that the raider simply rode away on a bicycle. There's no real proof, but if he did I find it hard to believe that his associates were also riding bicycles.'

'And?'

'I'm looking at the possibility that all the raids were done by the same man.' Bawtry touched his gold cuff-links. 'I've no direct evidence — it's just a feeling I have.'

Fallon drove hands into the jacket pockets of his crumpled blue suit. In fact, the suit was barely three months' old, but in less than that time Fallon somehow contrived to look like an unmade bed. He made a dry chuckle. 'A hunch, one of Sam's hunches. Not that they don't have a way of being right.'

Braxted, who had appeared to be studying his well-tended fingernails, looked up. 'The descriptions supplied by the banks concerned suggest that in each case there was a different raider.'

Brooker peeled the transparent wrapping from a small cigar, peering at it as if seeking enlightenment. 'I take it you have ideas about that, Sam?'

'The man who abandoned a bicycle in Liverpool 8 was seen going down towards Central Station. I went there and found strands from a wig in the lavatory.'

Ballinger's eyes flickered. 'Are you now saying that one man robbed each of the banks, adopting a different disguise in each case?'

'I'm not saying it as an established fact. I'm putting it forward as a tenable theory. No more, but equally no less, sir.'

'Fella would need more than a wig,' said Brooker. 'He'd need to change his facial appearance, his clothes — every damned thing about his outward appearance.'

'Yes, he would. But it can be done.'

'He'd have to be a ruddy expert to get away with it five times on the trot.'

Bawtry seemed about to speak, but he didn't. Instead, he waited.

Ballinger leaned back in his padded seat. 'Assuming for the moment that you're right, where does that take us?'

'I think we ought to go back to each of the banks and see if anyone can recall some point of linking identity.'

'All the witnesses have already been

re-examined — without any positive result.'

'They were seen before it occurred to me that we might be up against a single operator, sir. New questioning would be geared to the possibility that seemingly different men were, in fact, the same man every time.'

'Even if we establish that only one man was involved, it doesn't necessarily lead us to him.'

'Not immediately — but it would narrow the extent of our inquiries, give us a new and single focus.'

'If we knew what we were focusing on,' said Braxted. 'However, I can see the point — going on the assumption that the raids were all done by the same man changes the direction of the interrogation. Somebody may recall a point of common identity. I take it that's what you have in mind, Bawtry?'

'Yes, sir. If I'm wrong there's nothing lost because general inquiries will continue meantime.'

Ballinger pushed his chair back. 'Do it, Bawtry,' he said.

By two-thirty in the afternoon Bawtry had worked his way through three of the raided banks without so much as the hint of a clue. Nobody remembered anything which suggested that the raiders might be the same man in disguise and by the time Bawtry walked into the Mercantile and Oceanic Bank branch off Cheapside he was starting to doubt his own theory.

The manager, a stout balding man named Haslam, said: 'My staff, or those of them who witnessed the robbery, have already given detailed statements, but if there's anything else we can do . . . ' He let the rest of the sentence go unfinished.

Bawtry said patiently: 'With your permission I'd like to try a new approach, Mr. Haslam.'

'I see — or, rather, I don't quite see. I mean, what exactly do you have in mind, inspector?'

Bawtry thought of the old police routine: We ask the questions, you just give us the answers — we don't have to tell you why we're asking. But he decided against it. There were times when frankness paid off.

Aloud, he said: 'So far we've worked on the assumption that the robberies were the work of a number of men, possibly a gang. We're now looking at the possibility that only one man was involved.'

The manager stared. 'You mean one man changing his appearance each time?'

'Yes. It's no more than a theory at the moment — just the chance that one or other of your employees may recall something about the raiders's appearance which ties-in with the descriptions we have of the other men.'

Haslam pressed a desk buzzer. A tall man in his middle forties came in.

'This is our assistant manager, Mr. Lindley, but I believe you've met before.'

Bawtry nodded. 'How do you do, Mr. Lindley. I want to re-question Miss Frobisher — specifically about the physical appearance of the man who held her up at the counter.'

'I'll send her in,' Lindley said.

Helen Frobisher was thirty-five with a coolly composed manner, especially towards men, deriving from a broken romance four years previously.

Haslam said: 'Oh, Miss Frobisher — Inspector Bawtry would like to ask you some questions. Take a seat.'

She sat on the edge of a chair, stiffly — as if ready to spring off it, thought Bawtry privately.

'I don't know that there is anything I can usefully add to what I've already said,' she began.

'We're working on a new approach, Miss Frobisher. It's just possible you may be able to help us, without knowing it.'

Her pale blue eyes flickered momentarily. 'I don't think I quite understand.'

'Five bank robberies in five days. It seemed like the work of a gang because every man had a different appearance. We're now wondering whether all the raids were done by one man — in disguise.'

'Oh! I must admit I never thought of that.'

Bawtry smiled. 'Neither did we until today. Of course, we may be barking up the wrong tree. But it seemed worth while going into the possibility.'

'Yes, I see. But what makes you think I can help?'

'I don't know if you can, Miss Frobisher. It's just a chance that you may have noticed something about the man.'

'You mean some point of resemblance to the other men?'

'Yes.'

'But if the others were all different, inspector?'

'We'll have to see. The important thing is whether you can recall anything other than what you've already told us.'

'Like what?'

'Any distinguishing physical characteristic or mannerism — anything at all that you may have registered, even subconsciously.'

'Well, I don't know . . . '

'Try thinking back, right back from the moment this man came into the bank, Miss Frobisher.'

She didn't answer directly. Instead, she said: 'You'll have detailed descriptions of the other men — wouldn't it be helpful if I read them first?'

'Better not, at this stage. You might

unconsciously try to make the descriptions tally.'

For the first time a smile came on her face, banishing the slightly wary look. 'That's a good point. People do try to make recollections square with other recollections, don't they?'

'It has been known, yes.'

Helen Frobisher sat back for a moment with her eyes half-closed. When she reopened them she said thoughtfully: 'I took the man to be somewhere between thirty-five and forty. Tall, but not so tall as you are. About five-ten, well-made but not heavy. Thick dark-brown hair with a wave at the front. He had on a grey herringbone sports jacket and darker grey slacks. White shirt with a buttoned-down collar and a plain dark brown tie — narrower than the ties now fashionable. I remember that.'

All this had been in her original statement, but Bawtry merely said: 'Keep trying, Miss Frobisher.'

Her forehead puckered slightly, as if in concentration. Bawtry, who was standing, walked across the room and back. Then he said: 'His walk — anything you particularly noted about that?'

'Nothing, really — only that he carried himself well. I mean that he had a sort of purposeful way of walking. It showed on his face, too, and . . . ' Suddenly, she stopped.

'Yes?' Bawtry spoke softly, turning the single word into a question.

'I've remembered something. He touched the left side of his face three or four times with his index finger, as if something was irritating his skin, as if he might've cut himself shaving.'

'*Had* he nicked himself?'

'I didn't really notice. I've only just remembered about him touching his face.'

'Anything else?'

'I'm sorry, I can't think of anything.' She looked at Bawtry. 'What I've told you — does it help?'

'Not yet. It might do, though.' He turned to Haslam. 'Can I use your phone?'

'Of course.' The manager pushed the instrument across the desk.

Bawtry called the banks he had already been to. At two of them he drew blanks. But at the third the clerk who was held up said: 'Why, yes, that's right. I remember now — he kept touching his face, high up. I didn't see any mark. It was like a habit. Perhaps he wasn't aware that he was doing it.'

Bawtry put the phone down and exclaimed. He held out a hand. 'Thanks, Miss Frobisher — thanks for remembering.'

'I didn't until you questioned me, Mr. Bawtry. Does it mean they were one and the same man?'

'Unless there are two robbers given to scratching their faces — which seems improbable — yes.'

He drove to Headquarters, got out the list of cycle dealers and phoned them, one after the other. Nobody recalled a customer who kept touching his face. But Helen Frobisher had, also the clerk at the third bank. It was enough to be going on with.

Brooker came in, crossing the floor to where Bawtry was sitting.

Sam looked up sharply. 'What's happened?'

'I haven't said anything has.'

'Your expression is saying it for you.'

Brooker grinned. 'I'll have to wear the mask in future.' The grin went away. 'Another bank raid; a big one this time — and a murder and kidnapping to go with it,' he said.

8

Lynne Mayes turned her 1100 Escort into a cul-de-sac off North John Street and stopped outside the Transcontinental Bank behind a parked J-registration Viva pointing the other way. A uniformed police constable with his back towards her was looking at the Viva and she noticed the fact without any particular thought, unless whoever owned it hadn't renewed his Road Fund licence. She was having a day off and was on her way to the bank to draw some money.

In fact, she was about to get out of the Escort when a bearded man ran down the bank steps carrying a brief-case. He half-turned, then stopped dead in his tracks, staring at the Viva. The constable still had his back towards them.

The man with the brief-case swung back, wrenched open the offside of the Escort and slid in.

'Drive!'

Lynne's mouth opened but no words came.

The man swept his right hand in and out of his jacket, making an almost unseen blur of motion with a gun at the end of it.

'Make a normal turn. Just act naturally. Don't scream or yell for the cop or I'll give it you, no kidding. *Go on* — drive!'

He held the gun low down, out of sight, pressed into her side. Her hands were shaking, but she started driving. Shouts came from the bank entrance as she backed and turned.

Two clerks ran on to the pavement, going to the policeman. One of them speared a finger at the Escort. The constable jumped into the roadway, both arms outflung. Lynne swerved, braking. The nearside window was already wound down. The man beside her thrust the gun over the ledge and fired. There was a hard, snapping blast. The constable jack-knifed and went face down in the road, spreadeagled.

The man turned the gun back on her.

'Drive on, sweetheart,' he said. 'Left out of here, left into Water Street, then right. I'll tell you from there.'

She did what he said, mechanically, her mind in chaos. They passed the New Quay Tunnel entrance.

'Straight ahead, up the Waterloo Road.'

Out of the welter of her thoughts one surfaced. Someone would have taken the car's number. By now the police would be looking for it. Any minute now a police car would surge past them, its roof-light twirling, flagging them down.

As if reading her thoughts the man beside her said: 'The cops will be after us, if they've got the number — but they can't know which way we've gone.'

'They . . . ' Lynne stopped herself.

'They've got two-way radios. That's right, they've got radios. But with a bit of luck we'll be all right . . . and we'll be out of the car within minutes from now.'

They were just beyond the Clarence Dock power station when he said: 'Pull off the road into the open space on your left.' As he spoke he twitched off his false beard and the sunglasses.

She turned the car, stopped. Another thought numbed her senses: he's going to kill me, he'll kill me and simply walk away.

'Get out,' he said. 'I'll follow behind you. Just remember I'll be right behind you, with the gun.'

She got out, swaying slightly. She felt his arm steadying her. Then he was walking level with her.

'The gun's out of sight now, sweetheart, but don't think I won't use it, if I have to — or if you make me.'

She looked round wildly. They were on a dirt-surfaced demolition space. There was no one else there. But someone might appear in the distance. It didn't matter, though, did it? She would still have to do whatever he ordered.

He said: 'We're walking from here. Just a couple out walking, see? Link me — that'll make it look better.'

She put an arm in his. 'What do you want with me, where are we going?'

'A place near Stanley Drive, a little

bit of a place I've got, that's where we're going. As to what I want with you, you're what they call a hostage. I'd just as soon leave you here, but it's not on — you can identify me.'

'So can others.'

'I had the beard and specs on when I went into the bank.'

She had stopped trembling and was walking by his side, normally, marvelling that she could do it.

'Down here,' he said.

They turned into a short narrow street, a row of condemned terraced houses in the penultimate stage of dissolution: crumbling brickwork, smashed windows crudely boarded-up. A mangy cat sat forlornly on the rutted pavement. There was no other sign of life. The people who had once lived in the houses had long since gone, herded into high-rise flats or moved en masse into one of the new towns.

The last two houses were separated by a narrow entry. He turned into it. There was a door at the other end. He pushed it wide open and thrust her inside, ahead of him. The room was a kitchen with a brown stone sink. Unwashed pots were stacked in it. A heavy wooden table stood in the middle of the room, with two pitted chairs ranged against it.

'There's a bit of furniture in the living-room,' he said. 'Not much, but it'll do. I'll show you.' He opened an inner door, sagging on its hinges. The room had a musty smell. It also had a split horsehair settee and a bed. 'I dragged the bed down from upstairs — the only piece of furniture left in the place. You can have the bed or kip down on the settee — suit yourself.'

She shrank back involuntarily, looking at him with frightened eyes. He was a tall man with a smooth enigmatic face. He took out a packet of twenty Senior Service cigarettes.

'You want one?'

She shook her head dumbly.

He lit one himself, studying her. 'You're a pretty girl,' he said. 'But it's all right, I'll not touch you. I'm not a rapist or anything like that.'

'What do you want with me?'

'I told you — you're sort of a hostage. Well, perhaps that's not quite it. You're here because you're the one person who can identify me.'

'I don't know who you are . . . ' she began.

'You know what I look like, you could identify me, that's what.'

'So can the people in the bank.'

He grinned. 'I told you — they can identify a man with a black beard and tinted specs. And the cop had his back turned until he tried to flag us down.'

'You shot him,' she whispered.

'I had to then — there was just the chance that he may have seen through the disguise. Besides, he was in the way.'

'You shot him,' she repeated. 'You may have killed him.'

'Not may have, sweetheart. I had to make sure.'

A thought surfaced in her mind. She tried to banish it from her consciousness, but it was still there. My turn next . . .

The tall man said in a matter-of-fact tone: 'I took over this dump as part of the plan — to have somewhere to hide until the heat's off. Just for a few days. I had a car to make the getaway in, a car I took from a parking place. When I ran out of the bank the cop was looking at it. So I couldn't use it, I had to get in yours.' He grinned again. 'Lucky for me you drove up when you did. They'll not find us here, they'll not think of looking here.'

'You can't be sure.'

'No, not completely sure — that's where you come in as a hostage. I'd have to trade your safety for my escape. But there's not much chance of the cops finding us.'

'How long are you going to stay here?'

'No more than a few days — just time enough for the trail to go cold.'

'And then?'

'Then I'll be on my way — with £109,000.' He swung the bulky bag he was still holding. 'It's all here. Do you want to see it?' Without waiting for her to answer he opened the bag. She could see the money, stack on stack of money.

He dropped the bag in a corner of the room and said: 'I laid some food in — bread, butter, tinned stuff. Also some bottles of wine. It'll have to do. We can't cook — the gas and electricity are off.'

Lynne said weakly: 'I don't feel like eating.'

'There's tinned pilchards in the kitchen — open them,' he said curtly.

★ ★ ★

They were at the bank. The area was swarming with police. Brooker said savagely: 'Now it's not only a hold-up, it's kidnapping *and* murder.'

The street had been blocked off while chalk marks were made on it, where the body had been.

Ambulancemen had put the body on a stretcher. The police surgeon said: 'Shot through the heart, he died immediately. A .32 calibre bullet from an automatic.'

Brooker led the way into the bank. 'You ask the questions, Sam,' he said. 'I'll come in if I think of anything you overlook.'

A heavyweight balding man detached himself from the staff, moving forward.

Bawtry said: 'I take it you're the manager, sir?'

'Yes. James Allardyce is the name. I was in my office when it happened, but Miss Lee will be able to help you — she was directly involved. Miss Elizabeth Lee. Betty Lee to all of us.'

'And to me, then.' Bawtry smiled. 'Bawtry, Detective Inspector, with Chief Detective Inspector Brooker.' He held out a hand. 'Tell us in your own words exactly what happened.'

Betty Lee said: 'A bearded man with tinted glasses came up to my section. I didn't recall ever having seen him before. I had a sudden feeling that something was wrong. I don't know why, but that's what I felt. He had a sort of bulky bag. The next thing I knew he was holding a gun. I was . . . well, I was petrified. There was a lot of money lying around — in drawers and stacked behind me. He told me to get all of it and give it to him. I tried to shout to the other clerks, but he said if I uttered a sound he would shoot me . . . '

She smiled faintly. 'I couldn't have called out even if I'd tried — I seemed

101

to have lost the power of speech. I did what he told me, I had to.'

'Did none of your colleagues see what was happening, Betty?'

'Arthur — Mr. Burley, that is, he noticed and ran towards my section. The man told him to stay where he was if he didn't want to collect a bullet. He said that in as many words.'

'Go on,' said Bawtry gently.

'It was all over in moments — he just swept the money into the bag and ran out of the bank. I went faint — I had to hold on to the counter to stop myself falling.'

Bawtry glanced round. 'Did any of you run after him?'

Arthur Burley said: 'Three of us. I went first. The police officer was examining a parked car and had his back turned. The thief hesitated for a second, then jumped into an Escort which Miss Mayes had just driven up in.'

'You knew her?'

'Yes, Miss Lynne Mayes — a customer. She had just stopped the car outside the bank. I imagine she was coming in. The man got in the car and said something to her. Then the car began to move. I shouted to the policeman, who turned — and the man shot him, point blank. The next thing anybody knew the car had gone.'

Brooker said slowly: 'No suggestion that she was an accomplice?'

Burley blinked. 'I'm positive she wasn't. I saw her face as he jumped in beside her — it was chalk white.'

Bawtry fingered his plain gold cufflinks. 'The car the constable was looking at — do you think the raider arrived in it?'

'Yes, I had the impression. He went towards it, saw the officer and jumped into the other one. He was just lucky that Miss Mayes drove up at that time.'

George Lucas walked in. 'The car P.C. Lomax was examining was stolen from a car park first thing this morning. A description was put out on the radio. Bill Lomax must've spotted it.'

'It cost him his life,' said Brooker soberly.

Burley moved forward slightly. 'Miss

Mayes is a buyer for one of the stores in town.' He said which store it was, adding: 'She has a flat in the city centre, 9a Dorchester Close, near St. John's Precinct.'

Bawtry said thanks, though there seemed little point in going there. He turned to Betty Lee. 'The man had a beard and tinted glasses — did you think they were genuine?'

She hesitated, then said: 'I wondered about that . . . it did occur to me that they might not be.'

'What made you think that?'

'I just wondered if they were false. Especially the beard. I mean he wouldn't want to be easily identified, would he?'

Bawtry smiled. 'That's a perceptive comment, Miss Lee.'

She went on, surprisingly: 'I can draw you a fairly good likeness.'

'You can?'

'Yes. I took an art school course before I joined the bank. Do you want me to do it?'

'Yes, indeed.'

She picked up a quarto sheet of bond

paper and drew on it with deft, confident strokes. Burley, peering over her shoulder, exclaimed: 'That's him all right!'

Bawtry studied the representation for a moment, then said thoughtfully: 'Try it again — without the beard and the glasses.'

'The line of the jaw will be a guess, Mr. Bawtry . . . '

'Never mind, try it.'

She drew again, less confidently — but the result was better than she realised.

'It'll do,' Bawtry said. 'We'll have photo copies made and send them to the newspapers, locals and the nationals.'

Brooker jingled coins in his trouser pocket. 'Fella could be fifty miles away by now, but if the sketch appears in the big dailies someone may spot him.'

The telephone rang in the manager's office. Allardyce went in. He was back in less than a minute. 'Police Headquarters on the line — for either of you gentlemen.'

Brooker took the call. When he returned he said: 'That was Jenny Mycroft in the Information Room — Miss Mayes's car has been found abandoned up near the Clarence Dock. That could mean they've switched to another car. Damn.' He lit one of his small cigars, blew the match flame out and said: 'A squad of d.c.s and uniformed men have gone there, instructions to search the entire area. Might be lucky, but I doubt it.'

They drove back to Headquarters. Ballinger was waiting. He said tersely: 'It's murder now. Somehow we've got to apprehend the murderer before he gets too far away.'

'Yes,' said Brooker.

'Meaning exactly what?'

'Meaning I agree, sir.'

Ballinger's mouth twitched faintly. 'It's not pious agreement I'm looking for, Brooker, it's action.'

'There's already a squad of men in the area where the car was found — that's as close as we can hope to get at the present time. Not counting two hundred men searching the city.'

'Five bank raids in as many days, but this one caps them all.' Ballinger drove hands in his pockets. 'You, appear to be thinking about something Bawtry.'

Bawtry didn't answer immediately. Ballinger said, in a hardening voice: 'If you've any thoughts about this situation I want to know what they are.'

For a moment Bawtry felt irritation stirring, but he fought down the feeling and said levelly: 'I've no facts to support it — but it occurs to me that this latest bank job may be unconnected with the preceding ones, sir.'

'Oh, why?'

'The five raids on separate days involved relatively small amounts held in minor bank branches — and in no instance was violence committed, even though it may have been implied.'

There was a silence, then Brooker said softly: 'Sam has a point.'

Ballinger nursed his jaw. 'Your theory was that the five raids were done by the same man, changing his appearance each time. He could still be the man who shot P.C. Lomax and abducted Miss Mayes.'

'He could be, yes.'

'But you don't think he was?'

'I can't be positive, but the choice

of bank and the marked difference in the *modus operandi* at least suggest the possibility that in this instance an entirely different man may have been involved.'

Ballinger was on the point of speaking when the telephone rang.

Bawtry picked up the receiver. A remembered voice assailed his left ear.

'Smiler here. That you, Mr. B.?'

'Speaking. What can I do for you?'

Smiler Dobie chuckled fatly. 'It's more like what I can do for you, Mr. B. What's it worth?'

'Depends what you're selling, Smiler.'

'Information.'

'Such as what?'

'Something you'll be interested in hearing, especially at this time.'

'If it has anything to do with the bank jobs I could fetch you in for interrogation.'

'Yeh, you could, but I might not sing the right tune. On the other hand, you can have the information quick-like on the blower — say for twenty-five nicker.'

'I'll put a price on it when I know what it is, Smiler.'

Dobie manufactured a sigh. 'All right, I suppose that'll have to do.' He paused, then said: 'You fellas know anything about a villain known as Brad Tolman? Calls himself the King of the Blaggers.'

'A London villain wanted by the Yard for a bank hold-up and assault causing actual bodily harm. The hold-up went wrong. He didn't get anything, but he escaped. That was three months since and they're still looking for him.'

'They're not looking in the right place.'

'Go on . . . '

'They're looking for him down in The Smoke — only he ain't there. He's right here in the Pool.'

'You've *seen* him?'

'No, it's information on the grapevine. A tip-off from Lefty Halloran, what used to be up here. He thought we'd like to know on account of we don't go for competition from London fellas. Tolman's left London and Lefty says he's in Liverpool all right. The information's straight up, Mr. B. Is it worth twenty-five?'

'You're on, Smiler. I'm taking it you

don't know where he's staying?'

Dobie chuckled again. 'If I knew that the price'd be fifty quid,' he said.

Bawtry hung up and said: 'That was a local Ned named Smiler Dobie.'

Ballinger's eyes flickered briefly. 'A criminal, you mean?'

'A small time villain who sometimes acts as an informer. I undertook to let him have twenty-five pounds for some information.'

Ballinger's face registered distaste. 'I don't like using informers,' he said harshly.

'No, sir, but there are times when it becomes necessary.'

Brooker grinned. 'For twenty-five it'd better be good. I'm assuming it is, Sam.'

'I judge it to be. Dobie says that a known bank robber named Brad Tolman has left London for Liverpool. The Yard have been looking for him for months after an abortive raid in which Tolman seriously injured a clerk.'

'It's worth the twenty-five,' said Brooker.

Ballinger used the intercom to talk to Records. A civilian clerk came in carrying a buff-coloured file. Inside were two photographs of Brad Tolman.

Looking at them, Brooker said: 'Betty Lee did a good job drawing him without benefit of moustache.'

'Yes — someone ought to tell her, personally.'

Brooker grinned. 'Let Sam do it — he's better-looking than me.'

Ballinger, who rarely responded to facetiousness, said: 'We won't need the sketch now, we'll circulate copies of the photograph to the newspapers and television. Better just have the caption saying we believe this man may be able to help us with our inquiries. That'll be sufficient.'

Braxted, who had joined them, said tentatively: 'If Tolman is hiding in Liverpool — or anywhere else, come to think of it — having his picture in the papers is likely to keep him indoors.'

'Or emerging with a new disguise,' remarked Brooker.

'It's possible — but someone may have seen him. We can only hope.'

'And try,' said Ballinger. 'I want Tolman

arrested, and quickly, before . . . ' The unfinished sentence seemed to hang in the still air.

For a moment nobody spoke. Then Brooker said: 'The priority consideration is the girl, Lynne Mayes.'

'Yes, he may kill her. There isn't much time — if any.'

'We'll nail the bastard,' said Brooker. 'Sooner or later we'll nail him.'

'It had better be sooner. Pull out every stop.'

Bawtry said evenly: 'Before he went to London Lefty Halloran had friends up here, all of them dubious. Villains like Harry Franks and Bruiser Haggarty. They're still in the bailiwick. They may know something.'

Ballinger looked up. 'I take it you are acquainted with these men and know where they can be found, Bawtry.'

'Yes, sir.' Bawtry pushed his shirt cuff up to look at his watch. 'It's opening time. They'll be the first customers at the Green Man. The one on the Dock Road.'

'Then I suggest you add yourself to

the assembled company.' Ballinger's lean mouth made another small twitch. 'I hope it's not going to cost the department another twenty-five pounds,' he added drily.

'These two characters would shop their own grandmothers for three large Scotches apiece,' said Bawtry and went out.

9

The pub was squat and ugly, crouched on the narrow uneven pavement, another architectural hangover from another epoch. But the interior had been crudely tarted up and they had a new curved bar with a continuous brass footrail. When Bawtry walked in there were only two feet on the rail, belonging to Harry Franks and Bruiser Haggerty.

Their backs were towards him. Bawtry dropped a hand on each of their shoulders and said: 'Morning, Harry — you too, Bruiser.'

They had both stiffened. Harry Franks was the first to speak, screwing his head sideways. He was a slim, dapper man addicted to navy blue suits. Thirty-five years old and the last twenty years packed with experience, most of it regrettable.

Haggerty looked like what his nickname implied: a brutish minor prizefighter who had never got beyond preliminary bouts.

For the last decade he had been in and out of Walton Prison fairly regularly.

Franks got a smile out and hung it on his thin face. The smile looked as false as a backstreet money-lender's.

'Oh, it's you, Mr. B. — don't often see you in this boozer.'

Bruiser Haggerty said nothing eloquently. His eyes, which had a slightly glazed expression, glared.

Bawtry said amiably: 'You're only seeing me now because I want a word with you fellas and knew you'd be here.'

Haggerty drank noisily from a pint of black-and-tan, wiped his coarse mouth with the back of a hand, and said: 'Yeh? Me and Harry ain't done nowt.'

'I'm not accusing you two of any specific tort or malfeasance.'

The Bruiser sneered. 'What's that mean when it's at 'ome?'

'I'm not here to feel your collars, though I dare say it could be arranged if we dug deep enough. Some other time, happen.'

'You can get knotted, see?'

Harry Franks set fire to a cigarette, expelled a long stream of smoke and said: 'Belt up, Bruiser. This is a friendly visit, right?'

'I wouldn't set too great a store on friendship, Harry — but on the other hand I'm not here as an enemy.'

'Coppers . . . they're all enemies to the likes of us, that's what,' snarled Haggerty.

'The Bruiser's not himself this morning, Mr. B.,' said Franks pacifically. 'He got in a big boozing session last night and he's a bit fragile this morning.'

'Happen a large Scotch'll help, then — you, too, Harry?'

'I got no objection to supping with you, Mr. B. — but what's the idea?'

'I told you, I just want a few words.'

'What about?'

'A London villain named Brad Tolman.'

A look came on Harry Frank's face, fast and only briefly, but Bawtry saw it.

'Brad Tolman, eh?' Franks spoke with manufactured casualness.

Bawtry let his voice harden. 'If either of you know anything, no matter what,

116

about this fella I'll need to be told — right here and now.'

Tom Grimes, the landlord, drifted up the other side of the bar. 'Can I get you anything, Mr. Bawtry?'

'Two whiskies, large ones, for these comedians, Tom. I'll have a half of bitter.'

Grimes served the drinks. Three men came in and went down the other end of the bar, Grimes following.

Harry Franks said: 'We've heard of Tolman, right enough, but we ain't never met him. What d'you want to know for?'

'A man answering to Tolman's description robbed a bank earlier today. He got away with a pile of money. He also got away by jumping into a car belonging to a young woman.'

'You mean she was in it with him?'

'No, he forced her to drive him, kidnapped her — and shot a police constable dead in the street.'

'Jesus!' Harry Franks whispered the word, reached for the whisky and drank half of it in one.

When he put the glass down he said slowly: 'Like I just told you, we ain't never met Tolman . . . '

'But you know of him, you said as much. Do either of you know where he's likely to be in Liverpool?'

'I can give you the answer to that right away — it's no.'

'We'll try it another way. Do you know any fellas in the patch who are friends or acquaintances of Tolman?'

'The answer's still the same, Mr. B. — you got to believe us.' Franks paused, then went on: 'Lefty Halloran knows him, but Lefty left here for London a while back — so that's no use, is it?'

'No.' Bawtry eyed them levelly. 'But it's possible that Tolman knows somebody up here.'

Bruiser Haggerty said harshly: 'Maybe some fella or fellas here know Tolman, but it's got nowt to do with me and Harry.'

'You both get around — there's the chance that you might hear something.'

'We might, yeh,' Franks said. He drank the rest of his whisky and said: 'You want

118

us to ask around, is that it?'

'If you're willing.' Bawtry grinned faintly. 'Or even if you're not willing.'

Harry Franks turned an ornate signet ring on the third finger of his left hand, looked up and said distinctly: 'Murder and kidnapping are out of our line. Also, we don't like fellas from the Smoke muscling in up here. All right, then, we'll ask around — happen we'll find out summat. Mind you, Tolman could be a hundred bloody miles away by now, couldn't he?'

'It's possible but unlikely. The girl's car has been found abandoned near the Clarence Dock.'

'He could have had another waiting up there, Mr. B.'

'Yes, he could — but I think it more probable that he's taken her into hiding somewhere. If I'm right somebody may have seen him or even know where he's likely to be.'

'And you want us to ask around?'

Bawtry nodded. 'We've got a big police search under way, but there's always the chance that one or other of your friends

119

may know something that would help.'

'Okay, you're on. We don't go for violence, Mr. B. — you know that. I'm not saying we'll come up with owt, but if we do you get the info right away.'

Bawtry drove back to the bank. Betty Lee looked up with a quick smile.

'Anything else I can do for you, Mr. Bawtry?'

'I don't think so. I just dropped in to convey the thanks of the Assistant Chief Constable — he asked me to see you.' Bawtry explained, adding: 'The sketch you made was a pretty good likeness of this man Tolman.'

'Well, I'm glad I was able to help. How did you come to know about him?'

'From information received, Betty.'

She made another smile. 'That's a formula reply, isn't it?'

'Well, yes. I'll put it another way; we received information that this man had left London for Liverpool. There was a photo of him on the file. It occurred to us to compare it with your drawing — and the points of comparison were very specific, enough to indicate to us that Tolman is the man we want. He was involved in an abortive bank raid in London and is known to be violent.'

Betty Lee shivered. 'And he's abducted Lynne Mayes,' she said.

'Yes. From his point of view he had to because she can identify him.'

'So can I . . . '

'He doesn't know that and he won't know it because we're not sending copies of your sketch or your name to the newspapers — we're using the actual photograph.'

'Well, that's a relief, I must say.'

'Yes, he won't be coming after you. Not that I think he would, anyway — too risky.'

Betty Lee fell silent for a moment, then said: 'Lynne's parents ought to be notified, don't you think?'

'Yes — why, do you know them?'

She shook her head. 'No, but I know they live in Southport. Lynne mentioned them once. You'll probably find the address at her flat.'

'Thanks, I'll call there.'

'She has a boy friend, he lives in the same block of apartments near St. John's Precinct. As a matter of fact, she was supposed to be lunching with him today.'

'Why, did she tell you?'

'Yes, when she was in the bank the previous day. She was talking about him. He's an actor named Julian Arbor — in the rep company at the Riverside Theatre.' She looked at her watch. 'She was meeting him at twelve o'clock and it's now past one. He'll be wondering where she's got to.'

'I'd better see him,' Bawtry said.

Fifteen minutes later he parked his car on the forecourt and went into the small foyer. A neat compact man in his forties looked up from behind a walnut desk.

'Can I help you, sir?'

'I hope so. Are you the manager of the flats?'

'That's right. Burns is the name, Fred Burns. But if it's a letting you want I'm afraid we have no vacancies. All the flats have tenants.'

'I'm not after a flat, Mr. Burns.

I'd better introduce myself — Bawtry, Detective Inspector, Merseyside Police Headquarters.'

The manager blinked rapidly. 'Oh! I hope there's nothing wrong.'

'Unfortunately, there is. A bank hold-up. The man who did it shot a police constable dead in the street and forced Miss Lynne Mayes to drive him away in her car.'

'My God — you can't be serious.' The manager stopped, then said: 'That was a damned silly remark, of course you're serious. Has she been traced?'

'Not yet. We're doing what we can — two hundred officers are looking for her. Meanwhile, I'd like to have the pass key to her flat.'

'You want to search it, inspector?'

'Not exactly. I understand her parents live in Southport — I'm hoping to find their address.'

'Oh, I see.' The manager got out the pass-key. He hesitated. 'Do you wish me to accompany you?'

Bawtry smiled. 'Suit yourself, Mr. Burns.'

The flat looked as if it had been decorated the day before yesterday and the furnishing was stylish — very feminine, thought Sam. On the window shelf of the streamlined kitchen he found an envelope with a Southport postmark. He took out the letter and read enough to know that it was from her parents.

'This'll do,' he observed.

'And you say you don't want to search the flat?' Burns said it mechanically as if just to be saying something.

'There's no need. We're not trying to arrest Miss Mayes. We're trying to rescue her. Meanwhile, with your permission I'll use her telephone to notify her parents of what's happened.'

The telephone was in the lounge. He got through, trying to reassure her father and mother, not very successfully. 'I'll let you both know immediately we have any news, anything at all,' he promised.

A thought occurred as he put the receiver down. 'I understand that Miss Mayes is acquainted with another of your tenants, a Mr. Julian Arbor.'

'Oh? I didn't know that. But, then,

124

I probably wouldn't. Do you want to see him?'

'I think so, if he's in.'

'He may be, he works at night — he's an actor with the company at the new Riverside Theatre. On the other hand, he may have gone out. They often rehearse about mid-day. But we can try.'

The manager led the way and rang the doorbell. Nothing happened. He tried a second and third time. Nothing happened again. 'Must have gone out, I'm afraid,' he said apologetically. 'Did you want to question him?'

'No, just to let him know what's occurred.' Bawtry picked up the telephone and rang the stage doorkeeper, who said there was no rehearsal today.

'Probably gone out to lunch somewhere.' Bawtry reflected that by the time Julian Arbor returned he'd most likely see the story in the evening paper.

* * *

By shortly after 7 p.m. Tolman was getting restless. He stopped pacing the

125

decrepit living-room and said suddenly: 'I'm going out for a few drinks. I'll be back in an hour. Don't think you can get away because you'll be locked in, see?'

Her gaze went to the window, automatically. Tolman grinned. 'The windows have old-fashioned sashes and they're jammed tight. Better still, the windows are boarded-up.'

'How much longer are you going to keep me here?' she asked.

'Not long, perhaps only tonight. The coppers haven't been round this part, which means they haven't a clue as to where we are. If there's still no sign of them by tomorrow I'll be on my way, sweetheart.'

'You haven't a car now.'

'I could knock one off, easy — but I'll not bother. Risky, anyway. I'll simply walk to the station and catch a train — alone.' He said the last word with a kind of withdrawn inflexion.

Lynn fought down a rising panic within her, saying nothing.

He looked down at her dispassionately, then said: 'You'll be all right till I get back. You can't get out, I'll make sure of it.'

He locked the front door, then went out through the rear door, turning the key from the outside. He took the sack of paper money with him, suspended on thin straps round his neck, then covered it with a shabby off-white raincoat.

Lynne waited until his footsteps had faded. She looked through a chink in the dusty living-room window. There was no sign of life, nothing but desolation and blackened buildings on the brink of dissolution.

The panic fear she had experienced crystallised into silent words: He'll leave here . . . but he's going to kill me first, I know he will. He's killed once, he's nothing to lose. Oh God, somehow I've got to get out of here, I . . .

She stopped, her heart suddenly pounded as she flattened her face against the window pane. A small figure was silhouetted at the entrance to the deserted street. The figure moved forward, as if uncertainly.

It was the figure of a boy, a boy wearing

a red anorak and patched blue jeans. In a few more minutes he was level with the house. Lynne banged on the window, again and again.

The boy stopped, turning his head. He was no more than twelve years old, with an oddly vacant face.

She called out to him: 'Please . . . come here!'

The boy hesitated.

Desperately, Lynne called again: 'Please come and talk to me . . . I won't hurt you, I just want to tell you something. Come to the front door . . . '

He smiled, almost foolishly — but he came. There was a letter-slot in the door. The hinges were rusty, but she managed to get it open, put her mouth to it and said: 'I'm locked in — please can you get someone to let me out?'

'Eh? Wassup, then?'

'I've been locked in — please get some help.' She peered through the slot. The boy's face was still vacant. She realised, sinkingly, that he was mentally retarded.

He pushed at the door. 'It won't open,' he said. 'I'll have to go now.'

'Wait a minute . . . I'll give you a note. Take it to the police, or give it to your father and mother.'

'I'm not going home,' the boy said. 'I'm exploring, like.'

Lynne said steadily: 'I'll push the note through the letter slot. Give it to the first person you see — anybody. Please, will you do that?'

'Awright, but hurry. I got a lot of exploring to do.'

There was a letter in her handbag. She used the envelope to write: *I'm being held prisoner at a deserted house in a demolition area near the Clarence Dock, beyond Stanley Street. My name is Lynne Mayes. Please call the police — quickly.*

She poked the note through to him. 'You'll be able to tell someone how to get here, won't you?'

The boy didn't answer. He went on down the street.

10

Tolman walked to the Dock Road and found a boozer in a side street, a cramped shabby boozer but it would do. He would have preferred the bustle of a city centre pub, but he didn't want to be away for long. Suppose the girl started screaming? Let her. She was locked up in a condemned house in a totally deserted area, no chance of being heard. Just the same, better not stay more than half an hour or so.

The pub had vaults and a lounge bar, not that there was much difference between them, except the prices. He ordered a large Scotch with a half of bitter and glanced round the smoke-hazed room. There were a dozen people in it, nine of them men. The two women, both in their thirties, looked as if they might be on the game. Not that he was interested. With a fortune under his raincoat he could command the ministrations of the highest-priced prossies in the West End. The thought moved unbidden into his mind, followed by another: the sooner he got back to London the better. It seemed like a good idea to hide out in an abandoned terrace house in Liverpool until the heat was off, but now he wasn't so sure. The coppers would be combing the whole city for him and sooner or later they might get the idea of looking at empty derelict properties. But he had had to take the girl somewhere, hadn't he? If the uniformed cop hadn't been looking at the stolen car it wouldn't have arisen. Just a piece of unforseen bad luck. Still, he had got away with it. Only the girl knew what he looked like without the false beard. He'd have to do something about that . . .

Meanwhile, nobody in this pub knew him, or what he looked like without the beard. The police had probably put out an identikit picture of him — a man with a beard and tinted glasses and he no longer looked like that, did he?

He drank the double in two swallows, aware of the small fires starting up in his bloodstream.

'Same again, landlord.' He grinned. 'Well, I can't have the same again — similar, eh?'

'That's right, mate.' Sid Hawker got the drink, giving change for a £1 note. He was a sinewy man with a lantern-jawed face which looked as if it had been carved out of granite. He kept a chain-cosh on a shelf below the bar and had been known to use it — once breaking the forearm of a seaman who had mistakenly threatened him with a knife. It was that kind of a pub, though things had been quiet for some time.

Hawker leaned elbows on the bar, said conversationally: 'Ain't been in here before, have you?'

'No, I'm on a flying visit to Liverpool — business. I was expecting to meet a friend here, but he must be a bit late.'

'You talk like you might be from London.'

'That's right, though I've been here before. Not this pub, though.'

'Staying long, like?'

'Just a day or two.'

'We don't see many fellas from the Smoke, nearly all locals, or seamen, you might say.'

'That so?' Tolman spoke indifferently.

'Yeh, mostly. 'Scuse me.' Hawker drifted down the bar to serve another customer. The barmaid, a statuesque woman with rinsed crimson hair piled like a mad haystack, was drawing pints down at the other end.

Hawker served a pint of black-and-tan and came back. 'Don't often get strangers in here,' he said.

'No?'

'You're the first in a heck of a time. We're a bit off the beaten track, you know that.'

'I hadn't thought about it.' Tolman suddenly felt vaguely uneasy, but his schooled face gave nothing away.

'Last time we had a cockney in was nigh on two years since.' Hawker promoted a grin on his craggy face.

'The beer's better up here, so they tell me.'

'I only have the odd one, I'm a whisky drinker.'

Two more men came in. Hawker pulled two pints, then moved back along the bar and turned abruptly through a door into what looked like a small office. Tolman could see him picking up a copy of the *Liverpool Echo* from a desk. He stood there, looking at the front page. Then he toed the door shut.

Tolman froze. The barmaid nudged the door open. 'Sid — one of the pumps has gone off,' she said.

From where he was Tolman could see the landlord using the telephone. 'Shut the bloody door, Gladys,' he snarled.

Tolman stared round the bar. Nobody seemed to be paying him any attention. In a corner near the exit a middle-aged man was sitting at a table with a folded newspaper, not reading it. Tolman walked over and said blandly: 'Mind if I take a peep at your paper, guv?'

The middle-aged man looked up

owlishly. 'S'all right, wacker — help yerself.'

Tolman opened out Page One. A 42-point headline met his eye:

BANK RAIDER SHOOTS P.C. DEAD, KIDNAPS GIRL IN CAR

A bearded raider stole £109,000 from the Transcontinental Bank in Liverpool just after staff opened for business today, kidnapped a girl motorist and forced her to use her car as a getaway vehicle, then shot a police constable dead in the street.

The car, which belongs to Miss Lynne Mayes, a buyer in a city store, was later found abandoned near the Clarence Dock.

More than 200 police are combing the city looking for the raider and his kidnap victim.

Detectives believe that the killer was wearing a false beard.

There was more, but Tolman had read enough. A question rose in his mind: why did the coppers believe his beard was false? He got his answer as his gaze shifted to the photograph in another column. He ought to have seen it first, but he didn't.

'Christ!' Tolman said the word aloud. It was his photograph. The Liverpool fuzz must've got it from the Yard, over the wire, a telephoto copy. Yes, but how had they even connected him with the raid?

His lips moved, mouthing the caption: *Bradley Ronald Tolman, aged 43, a Londoner who may be in Liverpool. Police are anxious to contact this man who they believe can help with their inquiries.*

Like hell he could help the lousy jacks. But how did they know about him? Tolman let the paper slide down on the table. The near-drunk mumbled 'Thanksh, mate' as the landlord came through the small door behind the bar. His gaze went straight to Tolman.

He shouted: 'Hold that fella, some of you . . . '

A dozen heads jerked round, but nobody moved from where they were standing. Hawker dived for the hidden shelf, came up with the chain cosh and vaulted over the bar.

Tolman's right hand streaked inside his jacket to jump back holding a nine-shot Colt automatic.

'Better stay where you are, friend,' he whispered.

The landlord stopped as if an unseen door had slammed in his face. The chain cosh fell laxly against his side.

Tolman's gaze swept the silent room. 'Don't none of you get any ideas,' he said.

Nobody was having any.

Tolman backed out, kicked the door shut and pelted down the street and on into the Dock Road.

A squad car and a panda patrol were at the pub within minutes, but by that time Tolman had vanished.

★ ★ ★

The 12-year-old boy was Tommy Manley. He lived with his parents and a younger sister in Kirkby, another terrace house, but not yet under a demolition order.

A neat, tidy house with a father who was a good provider and a mother who looked after them, all the time, except that sometimes she had not been able to stop Tommy roaming around.

He seemed to have an almost uncanny instinct for the right time to slip out of the house. Dad and Mam worried about it, though he always came back, so far safe and sound though often dishevelled and muddy. They knew he was sub-normal, but they hadn't told the social workers for fear of having him put in care — a euphemism which, translated, meant taken away from them. This they could not face.

But this time they knew they were going to have to do something because Tommy hadn't come back.

Jim Mansley said: 'We'll have to go t'police, Mary.'

'Yes.' She said it tremulously.

Her husband put an arm round her shoulders. 'Tommy's never been late, not this late, before . . . summat could've happened to him.'

He could feel her body trembling. 'He

may have fallen and hurt himself,' he said, though that wasn't what he was thinking.

His wife said: 'Will they take him away from us?'

'Not the police, no love.'

'Council might . . . '

'Tommy's not mental, just a bit backward in school, but *they* haven't suggested taking him away. Any road, we've got to do something.'

'Yes . . . he might've been attacked. Dreadful things happen these days.' She started to cry.

Jim Manley said: 'I'll go to Police Headquarters. Tommy may have wandered out of t'district — it's better if I go to headquarters.'

Mary Manley dabbed at her eyes. 'Me and Jilly'll come with you, Jim.'

'We don't all need to go, love . . . '

'I don't want to stay in t'house alone, not knowing anything. We'll come with you.'

They got a bus into the city centre, then walked the short distance to Headquarters. Joe Oldfield, the uniformed desk sergeant, was on duty. Oldfield had been on the force longer than anybody. Young coppers, fresh out of cadet school at Bruche, were known to have suggested that he must be getting on towards a hundred — but not in Oldfield's presence.

He smiled as the Manleys came in. 'What's to do, then?' he said.

Jim Manley said: 'Our young lad, Tommy, is missing. He went out just afore teatime and hasn't come back.'

'How old is he?'

'Twelve last November.'

Oldfield reached for a foolscap report sheet. 'You'd better start by telling me your name and other details.'

'Jim Manley and this is my wife Mary and our daughter Jilly. No. 4 Roker Street, Kirkby. I'm a docker.'

Oldfield wrote it down, then said: 'I take it you don't have any idea where young Tommy could have gone, Mr. Manley?'

'No . . . ' Manley hesitated.

Noticing the hesitation, Oldfield said gently: 'Has he gone missing before?'

'He likes to go rambling, sir, that's a fact — but he always comes back.'

'Until this time?'

'Yes — that's why we're worried.'

'He just goes off — you've no idea where?'

Mary Manley said: 'He just tells us he's been for a bit of a ramble — exploring he calls it.'

'Have you told him not to do it?'

'Yes, sir — but he sort of slips out of t'house when I'm not looking. He never says where he's been, just exploring.'

Jilly Manley, a small girl with her hair in pigtails, said: 'Mam, I . . . '

'Be quiet, our Jilly,' her mother said.

'I just wanted to . . . '

'You can't go to t'toilet here.'

'It can be arranged, Mrs. Manley — I can get a policewoman to take her.'

'I don't want to wee,' the small girl said. 'I just remembered something . . . '

Oldfield looked at her. 'Something to do with Tommy, love?'

Jilly nodded. 'I just remembered something he said when he come in from school. He said he was going to

141

explore some old houses near t'dock.'

'Which one, love?'

'Some empty houses what are falling down, up near t'Clarence Dock, he said.' Her tilted nose wrinkled. 'Bagshaw Street, I think he said . . . '

She broke off as two uniformed constables came in, one on each side of a boy.

'Tommy!' His mother rushed towards him. 'Where've you been?'

'I just went for a bit of a ramble, Mam . . . '

'Your Dad and me have been half out of our minds with worry.'

'I'm sorry, Mam, I didn't think . . . '

Jim Manley said: 'Where'd you find him?'

Armiston, one of the two constables, answered. 'We spotted him wandering on some waste land near the Clarence Dock. We thought he looked lost and brought him in. We'd have driven him home but he didn't say where he lived, just that his name was Tommy. I take it you're his parents?'

Oldfield said: 'That's right — Mr. and

Mrs. Manley. They came here asking for us to help.'

Collins, the other constable, grinned faintly. 'I think he was scared of going home in case he got a belting from his old fella.'

'I've never laid a hand on him, sir,' Jim Manley said. 'I've threatened to, but I couldn't do it.'

'Dad's bark is worse than his bite,' Mrs. Manley said.

'Well, all's well then,' Collins suggested. 'It's lucky we were up there and saw him . . . ' He glanced round as Bawtry came in from the C.I.D. room. 'Evening, Mr. B.'

Bawtry looked at the group. 'What's happening?'

'We were out with the car near the dock looking for clues to the whereabouts of Miss Mayes. Instead, we found this lad wandering around on his own, so we brought him in.'

Oldfield said: 'In the meantime t'lad's parents had called asking for help — Mr. and Mrs. Manley. They were worried stiff.'

143

'I can imagine.' Bawtry smiled. 'You'd best take him home, I expect he's hungry.' He looked at the boy. 'Where'd you been, Tommy?'

'Just roaming — I like to go exploring.'

'It bothers your Mam and Dad when they don't know where you've gone — promise me you'll not do it again.'

'I promise, sir.'

'Where did you find him, Collins?'

'On some waste land near the Clarence Dock, Mr. B.'

The boy blinked. 'I wasn't there all the time, sir. I went exploring — down where them old houses is. I forget the name.'

Jilly Manley said: 'Bagshaw Street it was, like I said just now. He said as how he was going there.'

Armiston rubbed his chin. 'Bagshaw Street's a demolition zone — there's only a few terraced houses left in it and they're pretty well falling down.'

'Somebody lives in one of them,' Tommy said doggedly.

'There's only one or two still standing and they've been derelict for months,' Collins said. 'T'lad must've imagined it.'

144

'There was somebody there — I seen her. No, I didn't see her but she spoke to me. Through t'letter box . . . '

Bawtry said slowly: 'A lady spoke to you through the letter-box? Why didn't she open the door, Tommy?'

'She said as how it was locked and she couldn't open it.'

'Did she say who she was?'

'I can't remember. She just give me the paper.'

'What paper?' Bawtry asked patiently.

'The piece of paper what she wrote on. She asked me to give it to a policeman or to anyone I saw.'

'Have you still got it, Tommy?'

'I put it in me pocket.' He rummaged in his pocket and brought out the paper with two mint balls stuck to it.

Bawtry detached the mint balls, spread out the paper and read what was on it. He turned to the Manleys. 'Take your lad home, give him a good meal and don't chide him — he's done more than we've succeeded in doing.'

Jim Manley stared uncomprehendingly.

'By going exploring he's given us a clue

to a bank robbery and a kidnapping.'
Bawtry turned back to the two constables.
'Are you due back on a scheduled route?'

'As a matter of fact, yes.'

'You can scrub it. We're going out to
Bagshaw Street — Lynne Mayes is being
held prisoner there.'

'What!'

'It's in the note she pushed through the
letter-box. But hold on a few minutes
while I arrange for some more cars.'

Bawtry went through to Information.
Jenny Mycroft looked up inquiringly.

'Yes, Mr. Bawtry?'

'Radio all available cars to put a cordon
round Bagshaw Street. A total block. No
one to be allowed in or out. Lynne Mayes
is being held in one of the few remaining
houses there.'

'Right, Mr. Bawtry.'

Bawtry went back into the C.I.D.
room. Brooker was on the point of
leaving.

'What's up, Sam?'

Bawtry explained rapidly. 'I'm going
out with Armiston and Collins. We'll
probably be there first.'

'I'll come with you.' Brooker thought for a moment. 'We'd better go armed, Sam — Tolman may try to shoot his way out.'

Bawtry, who was a marksman, said: 'We'll need to be careful — he may kill her first. We'll have to try to get close without being observed.'

'It'll be a dicey situation.'

'Yes — we could take some CS gas canisters, just in case.'

'I'll fix it,' Brooker said.

Armiston drove them. Nobody spoke. Bawtry checked the mechanism of a .38 calibre revolver. Collins used the car radio to maintain contact with Information.

They were nearly there when he said: 'Squad cars and pandas moving into position, Mr. Brooker, awaiting further instructions from the command car — us.'

Brooker said: 'They're to ring the area at a distance, all lights out, while we decide. What do you think, Sam?'

'A dozen men strung out in a line approaching the house under cover of near darkness with instructions not to rush the place until we give the signal — a radio call for all car lights to be switched on in unison, beamed directly at the house.'

Collins looked uncertain. 'If we rush the place Tolman might shoot the girl.'

'I'll be *inside* the house. Drive straight past the end of the street and park on the waste land behind the house. We'll have a plain clothes officer knock on the door posing as someone from the housing department. Tolman will have to open the door or at least speak through it. Either way his attention will be diverted while I get in at the back.'

'Suppose the back door is locked?' Brooker said.

'In a derelict property it'll not be much of a lock.'

'He may have fitted a new one.'

'I'll get it open — and he'll not hear anything.'

Brooker grinned wryly. 'I'd forgotten you're an expert with locks. I remember now — a cracksman you once put down showed you all the tricks, didn't he?'

'Yes, it was a long time ago, but I haven't mislaid the knowledge.'

'You'll be taking a big risk, Sam . . .'

Bawtry shrugged. 'It's part of the job.'

They went past the street, turned on to the desolate land behind it, then stopped.

Bawtry said: 'Radio for a plainclothes officer to go up to the house. That'll give me enough time to get in at the back. When I get the lock open I'll give a single flash on a hand torch. That'll be the signal to rush the house inside the next five minutes.'

Collins said harshly: 'Lomax was a pal of mine . . . I'd like five minutes with the bastard who killed him.'

Brooker's face was expressionless. 'Physical violence will be used only if he resists arrest. Understood?'

'Yes, sir,' said Collins. 'Just the same . . .'

'There's no just the same, even if we share your feelings. Another thing, you're not armed and Tolman is. This could end in a shoot-out.' Brooker gripped Bawtry's hand. 'Good luck, Sam,' he said softly.

Bawtry stood still for a moment sighting the house, calculating distance and direction. There was just enough light to enable him to see. Then, abruptly, a low cloudbank moved in, blotting out the moon.

'Damn!' Now he had to rely solely on his calculations. He walked slowly, testing each footfall to avoid tripping over demolition rubble. Then, suddenly, light appeared in the rear of the house, a swaying light as if from a hand-held lamp. It stayed for a moment, then receded. Bawtry guessed Tolman had gone into the kitchen for something.

Reaching the house seemed like a minor eternity, though in fact it was no more than minutes. The rear door was at the side of the house. It was locked but not bolted. Bawtry manipulated a slim section of celluloid, felt the wards slide back. He edged the door inwards and stepped into the kitchen, waiting for his vision to adjust to the darkness. Then, as suddenly as it had come, the drifting cloudbank moved on, letting a pale lunar light in.

There was a door to his left. He stood against it, listening, holding the .38 with the safety catch off. Tolman was speaking.

' . . . got to leave you, sweetheart, now! I don't know how but the cops are on to me, they've put my picture in the bloody newspaper. So I'm leaving. I'll walk it to Lime Street and catch the late train to London, or to Manchester. It doesn't bloody matter just so long as I get out of Liverpool.'

Lynne Mayes said mechanically: 'They'll be watching the railway stations, they'll see you.'

Tolman made a brittle laugh. 'They'll be looking for me clean shaven or wearing a heavy beard and sunglasses. I won't look like that — I got some other disguise, just in case. They won't be looking for a man with thick grey hair and a drooping moustache.'

'What . . . ' Lynne hesitated. 'What about me?'

'You're the chief witness, sweetheart. That's too bad, I'll have to . . . ' He stopped almost violently as a sharp rap

151

sounded on the street door.

Bawtry palmed the inner door enough to get a slit view. Lynne Mayes was standing against the table. Tolman's back was turned. He started across the room to the front door. There was no hallway. Then he stopped, came back and pushed her ahead of him with a gun in her back.

'Who's there?' he called.

The plainclothes man who had knocked on the door said: 'From the housing department.'

Tolman breathed out audibly. 'What d'you want at this hour?'

'I'm making a survey in connection with the demolition order — yours is the last property to be seen.'

Tolman whispered: 'They don't send housing fellas round at this time of night. Bloody liar — he'll be a cop!' Loudly he called: 'Hold on while I open the door.'

He wrenched it open savagely, said: 'I've got a gun in the girl's back — make one move, any kind of move, and she gets it!'

The plainclothes man stood motionless.

Tolman said: 'Drop your gun. Right. Now kick it across the street.' He raised his voice. 'If you've got any mates out there they'd better stay where they are. I'm walking straight out with the girl. I want a car, the one you came in. Walk ahead of us, start the engine and then stand back. If anybody tries something . . . '

He never finished the sentence. Bawtry had kicked the inner door wide open and simultaneously flung himself headlong in a rugger tackle, low down.

At the same time the plainclothes man slammed Lynne Mayes sideways, out of line. Tolman's gun thudded to the ground. It didn't explode. He hit the rubbled ground with Bawtry on top. They rolled forward in a fighting mass, using every trick in the book. Tolman clawed for the gun, found it, jerked sideways coming up on his feet. A split second late. Bawtry was up first — with a tremendous short-arm punch to the solar plexus. Air gusted distressedly from Tolman's mouth as he jack-knifed. But he still had the gun and struggled partially erect to trigger it.

Bawtry feinted, brought his right hand down in a karate chop on the shoulder. Tolman's knees buckled, then he pitched forward, spreadeagled and unmoving.

Bawtry put a hand up to his mouth. Blood was seeping from it. Lynne Mayes swayed against him, sobbing. Headlights from a ring of cars suddenly blazed. Police swarmed in from every direction.

Tolman stirred. The plainclothes man who had knocked on the door put handcuffs on him.

Tolman looked at Bawtry. his eyes glaring madly. 'I'll kill you for this, copper . . . '

Brooker grinned wolfishly. 'You'll have to wait about twenty years,' he said.

11

Tolman was prowling the barely furnished interview room under the impassive gaze of a uniformed constable when Bawtry walked in.

'You might as well take a seat at the table, Tolman — we've got some talking to get through.'

Tolman's face was a silent snarl. He stood there his hands dangling at his side, not speaking.

'*Sit down!*' said Bawtry.

Tolman lowered himself into a straight-backed wooden chair.

'You can smoke, if you want.' Bawtry pushed a new packet of 20 Players across the table.

'I don't take anything off snotty jacks, I'll smoke my own.' Tolman felt in his jacket pocket, remembered that he had left his cigarettes in the derelict house and moved restlessly on the chair fighting the desire to smoke. The desire won. He

155

reached for the packet.

Bawtry's lighter flared. 'There'll be some tea along in a minute,' he said.

'Don't want . . . ' began Tolman.

'A smoke and a brew-up helps the conversation along.'

Tolman sneered. 'I got nothing to say to you, copper.'

'The name is Bawtry and I think you've plenty to say. A man in dead trouble usually has plenty to say and you're up to your ears in trouble, plural.'

'What's that supposed to mean?'

'More than one kind of trouble. But the biggest is murder.'

Tolman said: 'I just had a gun to scare the bank staff — when I got in the girl's car the gun went off accidentally.'

Bawtry beamed at him. 'You'll have to do better than that.'

'The girl accelerated. It made me jerk a bit and the gun went off.'

'The best defence counsel you can hire would have his work cut out trying that on the judge in the Crown Court.'

'I'm saying that's how it happened — and I want to see a lawyer.'

'It can be arranged — after we've had our chat. It may be a short chat or it may be a long one. Either way it'll be better for you to come clean.'

'I've got nothing to tell you . . . '

Bawtry said evenly: 'I want certain information from you. I can wait until the sun comes up and goes down again, if I have to.'

'You can — ' Tolman spat out a four-letter word.

'Basic Anglo-Saxon isn't going to do you any good, chummy. You're facing charges of robbery, kidnapping and murder — if you co-operate it might count in mitigation, up to a point.'

'Co-operation about what?'

'Specifically, the bank raids.'

Tolman dragged smoke from his cigarette. 'What d'you mean, bank raids — I only pulled one.'

Bawtry said patiently: 'That was the sixth raid — all done over a brief span of time. I want to know about the others.'

Tolman laughed stridently. 'You lousy cop — trying to pin more charges on me, as if you didn't already have enough.'

'We recovered £109,000 from the house you illegally occupied in Bagshaw Street. Before that there were five other bank jobs totalling more than £40,000. Where's it hidden?'

Tolman got a second sneer on his face. 'Forty grand for five jobs! You're looking at the wrong guy. I don't go for small time steals, I prefer to get it in one operation.'

'We've reason to think that the other raids were all done by one man wearing a different disguise each time.'

'You can think what you bloody like, but I'm telling you it wasn't me.'

Bawtry sat back. 'Also found in the house were a false beard, tinted glasses, a grey wig, a dark brown wig and two matching moustaches. Not enough to cover five different disguises, I agree — but maybe you have others somewhere.'

'Yes? Maybe New Year's Day comes in June.'

Bawtry went silent for a moment. Then he said: 'How long have you been in Liverpool?'

'Three days. I didn't want to stay at a hotel where fellas might remember me. A man I know in London told me about that area being demolished or ready for the bulldozer. I went up there and found this tumbledown house. It was as simple as that. I just walked in. I meant to hang on there for two or three more nights until the heat was off a bit and then scarper.'

It was feasible and Bawtry knew it. Where did that leave them? Right back where we started — with five totally unsolved robberies and not even the beginning of a clue as to who did them.

Tolman took another cigarette. 'I'd have got clean away with it if the coppers hadn't come. I still don't understand how you knew.'

'A young boy was out exploring the demolition zone. Miss Mayes called to him. She couldn't unlock the door — but she passed him a note through the letter box.'

'Christ!'

'Abducting Miss Mayes was as good

159

as signing a warrant for your own arrest — that and murder.'

'I had to snatch her and make her drive me on account of the cop looking at the car I stole for my getaway.'

'But for Lynne Mayes's presence of mind you'd probably have killed her, too.'

'I didn't do nothing to her . . . '

'You would have done — she's a principal witness.'

'Well, I didn't . . . and I didn't try anything sexually.'

'It hasn't been suggested, fortunately for you. Not,' Bawtry added grimly, 'that you could be in much worse trouble.'

Tolman said in a voice which only just reached Bawtry: 'I'll likely get life with a fifteen or twenty-year recommendation, won't I?'

'Happen.'

Tolman's hard mouth moved in a travestied smile. 'I'll be too old to bother about trying to kill you then. I didn't really mean it, anyway. I just said it. You were just doing the lousy job they pay you for in peanuts, I guess.'

Bawtry said: 'Have you ever lived in America?'

'I was there a couple of years, why?'

'It was the way you spoke a moment ago. What made you come back to England?'

'I was in Detroit, which is one tough city for crime. I got in with one of the mobs. I was making out all right until I found the cops were nearly breathing down my neck. I didn't wait for them to feel my collar — I caught the next plane back to dear old Blighty.' Tolman grimaced. 'I might've done better to have stayed on. I couldn't have done worse, the way it's turned out.'

Bawtry said: 'How are you going to plead — and you don't have to answer that.'

'I don't mind — not guilty to murder, guilty to manslaughter, guilty to the bank job and the kidnapping, but the latter being done merely to make my getaway.'

The way things are this character might get away with manslaughter, Bawtry thought. Aloud, he said: 'One more thing — do you have any knowledge whatever of who could have done the five other bank jobs?'

'None. I wish I had . . . it'd make it that much better for me. But I've told you all I know, there isn't any more. For God's sake, it's enough,' Tolman added bitterly.

The uniformed constable took Tolman back to the cells. Bawtry walked slowly into the room jointly tenanted by Braxted and Fallon. Ballinger was also there. A moment later Brooker came in and sat, as usual, with his hands dangling between his knees.

'Well, Bawtry?' The question came from Ballinger, sharply.

Bawtry said: 'Tolman denies murder sir. He claims the gun was discharged by accident when Miss Mayes accelerated. He says he will plead guilty to manslaughter.'

'Lying bastard,' said Brooker.

Ballinger said dispassionately: 'Go on, Bawtry.'

'For the rest, Tolman admits abducting Miss Mayes, saying he had to do it to make his getaway because Lomax was examining the car Tolman had stolen. He will also plead guilty to the bank robbery today.'

Braxted leaned forward, drumming fingers on his desk. 'What about the five other bank robberies?'

'Tolman denies having anything to do with them, sir.'

Ted Fallon drove hands into the sagging pockets of a navy blue suit. He eyed Bawtry and said: 'What do you think, Sam?'

'I think Tolman is a right villain who would try to lie his way out of anything, but on this point I'm inclined to believe what he says.'

'I'd like footnotes on that,' Ballinger said.

Bawtry got cigarettes out. 'All the money stolen in the latest raid has been found in the house Tolman was hiding out in, together with some wigs. The disguises aren't enough to cover the five previous raids — and, even more to the point, we've discovered no trace of the proceeds from the earlier robberies. In a sentence, I don't think Tolman had anything to do with them, sir.'

'Chummy could've put the other money somewhere else' Brooker said. He lit a small cigar, blew out the match flame, adding: 'I'm willing to concede that it's unlikely, though.'

'How long has he been in Liverpool, or don't we know?' queried Braxted.

'He claims three days and nights. He says that someone down in London told him about demolition areas and that he found this one and moved into the house, reckoning it'd be safer than booking into an hotel.'

'From his point of view that makes sense,' mused Brooker. 'Not that I like accepting anything Tolman says. True, we've got him on major charges — but he *could* have posted the other money to himself in London — even to an accommodation address. On the other hand, as I said, we didn't find enough disguises to cover five different impersonations. Also there were complete changes of clothes for the other robberies and Tolman only had what he stood up in.' Brooker exhaled a stream of blue smoke. 'I go along with Sam on this,' he said.

For a moment nobody spoke. Then Ballinger said quietly: 'It looks that way. I want every effort made to test this man's claim — but it looks that way. If so we're back where we started so far as the first five robberies are concerned.'

Fallon's overlong face crumpled in a near smile. 'The Chief Con. won't be pleased.'

'He'll be pleased that we've solved the raid today and the abduction of Miss Mayes — but he'll be pressing for results on the other raids.'

'We're looking for five distinctly different villains or one man playing all the parts,' said Braxted. 'Either way we've got plenty on our hands.'

'Yes.' Ballinger rose as he spoke. 'It may serve a purpose if we go right back to the beginning — something, perhaps something unforseen or over-looked at the time, may come up.' He looked at his wrist watch. 'It's been a very long day for you all. I suggest sleep — and a completely fresh start in the morning.'

Brooker and Bawtry walked into the C.I.D. room. Brooker grinned. 'Sleep! I could use some, but not until I've been to the Press Club. Coming?'

'I'm going home, but thanks all the same. Carol's back.'

'If she was waiting for me I'd be going home, too,' said Brooker.

★ ★ ★

Julian knew Lynne had been kidnapped well before the time set for their lunch date. He heard it in a news flash on local radio — and passed the next few hours in a torment of indecision. Not because he didn't know what he ought to do; he knew well enough that he ought to contact the police for information. But with £43,000 of stolen money hidden in his flat even the thought of telephoning Headquarters almost literally petrified him. The police didn't know he was friendly with Lynne. Why go out of the way to tell them, at least at this stage?

Better to wait . . . or was it? Sooner or later they would have to know, wouldn't they? No, it didn't necessarily follow. In any case it was still better to wait. Don't rush fences, don't get involved with the law until you have to. Besides, the police might find her within hours. They didn't know he had a lunch date with Lynne or even that he knew her. Stay out of the picture, don't walk into it unless you have to . . .

Suppose the police found her quickly and she mentioned him? The back of his neck went wet with sweat, cold as a dog's nose. He pulled himself together. Don't panic, chum. The fact that you know her doesn't link you with the bank raids. Just the same, keep out of the coppers' way for the time being. Give them the chance to find her first.

As the thoughts milled in his mind Julian realised that his preoccupations were exclusively concerned with himself. He forced himself to think about Lynne. She might be dead by now — the kidnapper had already killed a police officer, another killing wasn't going to make much difference. Dear God, I hope it hasn't gone that way.

Another reflection surfaced in his mind: the police would probably associate the unknown bank raider with the other robberies. He'd deny it, of course, if he was caught — but he might not be caught, not immediately, anyway, and in the meantime the full strength of police investigations would be concentrated on him, not on Julian Arbor.

He went out, walking aimlessly, killing time. He couldn't face a restaurant lunch. Instead, he ate a beef sandwich, accompanied by a large Scotch, in a bar near the theatre.

Don Perry, a member of the repertory company, came in. 'Hi, Julian I didn't know you lunched here.'

'I don't as a rule,' Julian answered, 'But I've an appointment this afternoon and just dropped in for a sandwich. What'll you have?'

'Pint of bitter, I think. You should've tried one of the hot snacks they serve here — they're pretty good.'

'In a bit of a hurry, so I settled for the beef sandwhich.'

The bitter came. Perry drank some of

it and said: 'How do you like the way things are going at the theatre?'

'Everything seems to be going fine.'

'That's a fact. We're getting some damned good plays and the box office is doing a roaring trade.'

'So I gather.' Julian forced himself to smile. 'We'll all have to put in for a rise, eh?'

'That's an idea — except that we've all signed contracts — still, no harm in trying. Meanwhile, it's nice to be in a company doing good business. Suits me even if the management don't give us a rise — I'm thankful to be with a long-run company.'

'Yes, it certainly makes a change.' Julian spoke almost absently.

Perry noticed it. 'Something on your mind, Julian?'

'I don't think so — what makes you ask?'

'You sounded sort of faraway just then.'

'Oh, that? I was mentally running through some of the lines in the play we're reading. Some dialogue in the third

169

act — I don't think I'm getting it just right.' It was a lie because he never had trouble with his lines.

Perry grinned. 'Well, that wants chalking up. You have a reputation for always being on time and word-perfect.'

'You flatter me.'

'No, seriously, that's what the others say about you.'

'Well, I know the lines all right — it's just a question of getting the right emphasis.'

'Don't worry, you'll be all right on the night as they say.'

'I hope so.'

'The day you fluff a line that'll be the day,' said Perry. 'Will you have another drink?'

'Thanks all the same but not now. I've got this appointment.'

'That leaves me owing you one.'

Julian manufactured a smile. 'I'll sue you for it, then.'

'We could have a couple after the show — if the pubs are shut we can go across to the Press Club. I've just become a member.'

'Yes, we could do that. Well, see you, Don.'

He went out of the bar, passed more time aimlessly walking, finding himself at the Pierhead without any clear idea of how he got there. He stood for ten minutes by the Princes landing stage, trying to still the turmoil in his mind. Slowly, he regained some composure, turned and made his way towards Church Street. Finally, he went back to his flat, made himself coffee and got out the script of the new play. It wasn't necessary because he knew it — every line, every nuance. But it got him through the rest of the afternoon until it was time to go down to the theatre.

The company took four curtain calls and the director said: 'Congratulations, Julian — that's the best performance you've ever given.'

He had known that while he was doing it, marvelling at the fact; perhaps having inner trouble helped? No, more likely the other way round: the demands of the play had muted the inner tension.

'Thanks for the compliment, John,' he

said. 'But I thought everybody was on form tonight.'

'They were, but your performance was outstanding. Come along to the theatre bar and I'll buy you a drink.'

'They'll be closing, won't they?'

'Not for ten minutes, and I dare say we can persuade them to let us stay on for a short while.'

Don Perry came up. 'I'm supposed to be taking Julian to the Press Club, but we can go on there later. By the way, have you heard the news?'

'What news?'

'I heard it on the radio in my dressing-room. About the bank raid and the girl who was kidnapped . . . '

Despite the backstage warmth Julian went cold, but his actor's training schooled his voice as he said: 'Oh? I haven't been listening to the radio.'

'It's in the evening paper — about the hold-up and the kidnap. The fellow who robbed the bank shot a copper dead and forced a girl to drive him away. I switched the radio on a few minutes ago and it turns out the police have caught him and freed the girl. Pretty swift work. A girl named Mayes — Lynne Mayes I think it is . . . what's the matter?'

'Did you say her name was Lynne Mayes?' Julian pitched his voice at just the right degree of concern.

'That's right. She had just left the bank when the hold-up fellow dashed out and made her drive him.' Perry stared. 'You look as if you'd just seen a ghost, Julian.'

'I know her. She lives in the same block of flats as me. I mean I know her personally. My God — is she all right?'

'I think so. Suffering from shock, though. They're keeping her in hospital for a night — just for observation. It was mentioned in the newscast.'

'Which hospital?'

Perry told him.

Julian said thickly: 'I'll have to miss drinks with you both. I'll drop in at the hospital to see how she is.'

'I didn't know you were friendly with her.'

'I didn't know she had been abducted. She's a friend of mine. Look, I'll get my make-up off and join you in the bar.' He was already moving as he spoke.

A few minutes later Perry put his head round the dressing-room door. 'Ready, Julian?'

'Yes.' He lit a cigarette and picked up his raincoat.

There was a folded copy of the *Liverpool Echo* on the dressing-table and Don Perry noticed it.

12

Carole was waiting for him when Bawtry got back to the flat they occupied within walking distance of Police Headquarters. Bawtry had lived there as a bachelor and Carole liked it, perhaps partly because this was where they first went to bed together the night before they married by special licence.

Now she came from the lounge across the small hall and straight into his arms. Then, disengaging herself, she said simply: 'I missed you, Sam.'

'I missed you.'

'You're late home, though.'

'Something cropped up.'

'Something important, you mean?'

'Yes, it began with a young boy going missing, but it turned out to be something very much more than that.'

'Do you want to tell me?' She knew that most policemen rarely talked about their work in the privacy of their homes;

it was a kind of unwritten rule. But with her Sam sometimes broke the rule, the way he often threw away the book in handling a case.

'Yes,' he said. 'I'll tell you, love.'

She listened in silence, only betraying emotion when he described what had happened at the condemned house.

When he had finished she said: 'You could have been killed.'

'I kept that risk right down by getting in at the back while one of the other lads knocked on the front door.'

'If this man Tolman had turned he would probably have shot you.'

'You're forgetting that I was armed, too.'

'Would you have used the gun, Sam?'

'To save my life or the life of Lynne Mayes — yes. But the way we played it the situation didn't arise.'

'I'm glad.'

'You wouldn't like to be married to a man who had killed someone?'

She touched his sleeve briefly. 'I didn't mean that. I know you wouldn't kill anyone unless it was in self-defence. I'm just glad you didn't have to do it.'

'I'm not sorry either. Taking a fellow human being's life is the ultimate thing. I'm glad it wasn't necessary. Not that Tolman's life is anything to write home about. He killed Lomax — a man he had never even seen before — in cold blood.'

Carole said: 'I don't know how anyone can do that.'

'It's happening all the time just now.'

'I know. What's happening to our country, Sam?'

'A new climate of violence, unwittingly accelerated by platoons of liberal do-gooders.' Bawtry smiled faintly. 'But you don't want a recital of my views on that, do you?'

'I didn't go along with your views at one time, or not all of them. I felt that people who got out of line needed care and rehabilitation. I still think some do — but they're a diminishing number. Too many crimes of violence . . . the muggings, the hold-ups, even old ladies being attacked and tortured, sometimes by kids scarcely in their teens.'

'The way things now stand we're

creating a race of juvenile criminals the law can't touch — not in any retributive sense.'

'It's wrong, Sam. The priorities are all wrong. Concern for the offender ought to take second place to concern for the victims. I didn't always see it that way, but I see it now.'

'If there was a referendum you'd find that the majority of ordinary decent folk would say the same. But they're not consulted. Meanwhile, we have leniency amounting to softness in some of the courts. As to the do-gooders, they don't have to see the victims of violence . . . we do.'

'This used to be the most law-abiding of countries. The change that's come about in recent years frightens me.'

Sam said slowly: 'In the middle of the war, with every town and city blacked out, you could walk the streets at night and nobody would touch you. Now it's not even safe in broad daylight. Like today when Constable Lomax was shot dead in the street. And the man who did it won't pay the ultimate penalty.'

'Do you really believe that capital punishment would cut the crime rate?'

'It'd make that kind of villain think more than twice — that I'm willing to bet on.' Bawtry smiled faintly. 'But enough of that.'

'Meaning you're hungry? I'll get something for us.'

'No, you won't. I'm going to take you out for dinner.'

'It's getting late . . . '

'Not too late — no shortage of late night restaurants. There's a good one near the new Riverside Theatre. I'll book a table now.' He picked up the telephone.

'If we're going out to eat I'll have to change.'

'You look smashing the way you are.'

Carol laughed. 'You'd say that no matter what I had on. I'll change into a dress — it won't take me long. You can fix yourself a drink while I do it.'

'All right.' Bawtry wasn't a drinking man, unlike Brooker, but he had a small Scotch to pass the time. The wait wasn't long and about twenty minutes later they

179

were in the restaurant.

The head waiter came up. 'Mr. and Mrs. Bawtry?'

Sam nodded.

'Lucky you telephoned sir. You got the last available table. Mr. Arbor usually has it, but he's not in tonight.'

The name rang a small bell in Bawtry's mind. 'Would that be Julian Arbor, the actor?'

'Why, yes — do you know him?'

'I know of him, but we haven't actually met.'

The head waiter showed them to their table. 'Mr. Arbor dines here two or three times a week, sometimes more than that . . . ' There was a small hesitancy, then: 'Are you Inspector Bawtry?'

'That's right, though I wasn't aware you knew me.'

'Somebody pointed you out to me once and I have a good memory for faces. I hear you've caught the bank raider. It was on the raido.'

Bawtry nodded briefly.

'I gather the young lady is safe. Miss Mayes — she's been in here for dinner a few times, with Mr. Arbor. The radio said she is in hospital. Just for a check-up, it said.'

'That's right, an overnight stay, that's all.' Bawtry recalled that Lynne hadn't wanted to go into hospital, but the doctor advised it.

They were half-way through the first course when Carol said: 'Has Julian Arbor been in touch with you?'

'As a matter of fact, no. A girl clerk at the bank told us that Miss Mayes was going to have lunch with him, but she couldn't have done, I called at Arbor's flat, but he'd gone out.'

'You'd have thought he would have been worried at her not turning up.'

'Well, I don't know. They live in the same block of flats. He probably called on her, found she wasn't in and concluded that she hadn't been able to make it. Unless he had the radio on or bought the evening paper he wouldn't even know about her being abducted.'

'I suppose not . . . ' Carol said the words slowly.

'Why, what's on your mind?' Sam asked.

'Nothing really, except that I'd have thought he would be in touch with the police. No, that's not right,' Carol went on with feminine inconsistency. 'If he didn't know about the bank raid and the kidnapping there wouldn't be any reason for him to contact you.

'No, there wouldn't.'

'It's funny, though.'

'How?'

'Well, I'd have expected him to do something — I don't know just what, but something.'

'If he didn't know what had happened to her there wouldn't be any reason for him to be concerned.'

'You'd be concerned if I promised to meet you for lunch and then didn't turn up, wouldn't you?'

'Yes, I would.' Bawtry poured white wine, returned the bottle to the ice bucket and said: 'Happen he's not the worrying kind and simply thought she couldn't make the date.'

'After all this time he must've heard what happened.'

'If he has he's probably either phoned the hospital or gone there.'

'Yes . . . I didn't think of that. Anyway, it's not really important, is it? I mean you've caught the bank robber.'

'The blagger,' said Bawtry with a grin.

'That sounded like a swear word.'

'Police and underworld slang. A blagger isn't just any kind of villain or Ned — but, very specifically, a bank robber. The description fits Tolman like the proverbial glove.'

'Well, he certainly seems to have committed enough bank robberies in the last week or so, doesn't he?'

For a moment Sam didn't answer. Then he said slowly: 'To tell you the truth, I'm not so sure about that.'

'You mean he denies it?'

'Yes, but that's not the reason or not the whole reason. I've a feeling that the lesser robberies were the work of someone else.'

'Several men, you mean?'

'Not necessarily — we're looking at the possibility that they were all done by one man who kept changing his appearance.'

Bawtry sketched the background of their inquiries.

Carol said: 'If it was one man constantly disguising himself he'd need to be an expert at it.'

'Yes, he would . . . ' Bawtry fell silent again. A barely formulated thought stirred far down in his mind. It was too far-fetched.

But it was still there when they went to bed. Then, with Carol in his embrace, he dismissed it.

★ ★ ★

It was a minute after 11 a.m. next day when Bawtry thumbed the doorbell of Julian's flat. Mellow chimes sounded, then the pad of footsteps and the door opened.

Julian was still in pyjamas with a crimson dressing-gown over them.

'Yes?' he said.

'Bawtry, Detective Inspector, Merseyside Metropolitan Police . . . ' As he spoke he noticed a sudden, fleeting expression on the other's handsome face. It didn't

184

signify anything. Just a passing expression, immediately banished by a smile. But it had been there.

'Are you Mr. Julian Arbor?'

Julian nodded.

'I'd appreciate it if you could spare me a few minutes, Mr. Arbor.'

A zero emptiness gripped Julian, like a signpost on the route to panic. But his was a face schooled in a cavalcade of disparate acting rôles and from the repertoire he chose a look of bland inquiry.

'I'm happy to meet you, Mr. Bawtry.' He palmed a hand over thick hair only tentatively touched with grey. A smile, then: 'Perhaps I should add the question — to what am I indebted for the honour of this visit?'

'Just a routine visit, Mr. Arbor, concerning a young lady with whom I believe you are acquainted.'

'You mean Lynne — Miss Mayes — I take it.' Julian held the door wide open. 'Do come in, Inspector.'

Bawtry walked into the living room. Julian said: 'Would you like coffee — or perhaps something stronger?'

'Coffee will do admirably, if you're making it.'

'As a matter of fact, I was about to do just that. Come into the kitchen.' He set out another cup and saucer alongside the coffee drip. 'You *have* come about Lynne?'

'Yes. It's really a courtesy call . . . unless you are already in possession of the relevant facts.'

'I saw her in hospital last night. I went as soon as I heard the news — a shocking business.'

'She's coming out today, I understand.'

'This afternoon. I'm going for her at two-thirty.' Julian poured the coffee. 'My congratulations, Mr. Bawtry, on the way you and your officers handled the incident.'

'We had a certain measure of luck — a young boy who was roaming round a demolition zone approached the house where Miss Mayes was being held prisoner. Better still, Miss Mayes passed him a note.'

'Yes, Lynne told me. Just the same,

your department acted with the most commendable speed. But for that Lynne might have . . . ' Julian left the rest of the sentence unspoken.

Bawtry finished it. 'She might have come to serious harm. The man who abducted her had already killed one of our officers.'

'He might have murdered Lynne to prevent identification?'

'It's a strong probability. When did you hear the news of the kidnapping, Mr. Arbor?'

'Not until quite late in the evening — immediately after the show, as a matter of fact. I'm an actor with the repertory company at the Riverside Theatre, but you probably know that?'

Bawtry nodded. 'A young lady employee at the bank said Miss Mayes happened to mention that she was lunching with you yesterday.'

'We had a lunch date, yes.' A new panic assailed him, but he added composedly: 'I assumed she couldn't make it due to business.'

'You didn't call to find out?'

'Well, no. Perhaps I should have done — but I simply took it that something had arisen to prevent her. Her flat is in this building, so it would've been easy for me to call — but I took it that she had been unable to keep our date.'

'The bank robbery and Miss Mayes's kidnapping were on the local radio and in the evening paper, but you missed it?'

'Unfortunately, yes. I didn't have the radio on and I missed the evening paper, I'm afraid.'

'I see. How *did* you get to know what had happened?'

'Don Perry — a colleague of mine — told me. It was a shock. We were supposed to be going for a drink — but I rushed out to the hospital instead. I was in something of a state, I can tell you. I wish now that I'd called at Lynne's flat before lunch.' Julian made a small gesture. 'On the other hand, it wouldn't have helped, would it? I mean she wasn't there.'

'No, by that time she was being held prisoner in the condemned house on the demolition site. Luckily, she wasn't harmed in any way.'

'Thanks to the police . . . ' Julian paused, then said: 'Knowing that we had a lunch date you probably expected to hear from me during the day?'

'The thought did occur, Mr. Arbor — but it turns out that you were unaware of what happened until late last night. That clears it up.'

Julian smiled faintly. 'In the event I'm glad I didn't know — I'd have been half out of my mind with worry all day.'

'I can imagine.'

Julian said: 'I suppose you'll want to take a statement from Lynne?'

'It'll have been done by now — Detective Sergeant Lucas went to the hospital this morning. Incidentally, you'll be happy to know that Miss Mayes seems to have fully recovered from the shock of her ordeal.'

'That's great. If she feels up to it, I'll take her out to dinner after the show — the most expensive meal they can put on.'

'Yes, you owe her that,' said Bawtry smilingly. 'Well, thanks for talking to me.'

'Glad to, Inspector. Not that I've been any help.'

'You've cleared up a minor point, Mr. Arbor.'

'Very minor. The main thing is that Lynne is well — that and the fact that you've caught the bank raider.'

'Yes.'

'He must be the same fellow who robbed the other banks, then?'

'Except for the fact that the only money we found was from the hold-up yesterday.'

'He could've hidden it somewhere else, couldn't he?'

'It's a possibility we're not ignoring. But we're also looking into the possibility that the earlier raids were the work of someone else.'

'Really? I'd have thought the circumstances pointed pretty conclusively to this chap Tolman.'

'They do, on the face of it.'

'Someone else sounds like a bit of a long shot.'

'It does, but long shots sometimes come off. Well, thanks again, Mr. Arbor.'

Bawtry held out a hand. He noticed that Julian's felt cold, though the day was warm.

13

Julian went into the living room and poured himself a stiff brandy. He was not a drinking man, least of all in the daytime, but now he needed a drink. It didn't help, though. When he had finished it the fear was still with him. He tried to reason himself out of it — but the recollection of Bawtry's closing remark was still there. 'We're also looking at the possibility that the earlier raids were the work of someone else . . . '

What if they were? It didn't mean the police suspected him, did it? It *couldn't* mean that. He had left not so much as the vestige of a clue, he was completely sure of that. There was nothing to fear. He told himself that over and over again, but the sensation of fear refused to go away. Why had this Detective Inspector called? He had said it was a routine visit, but he didn't look the kind of man who did anything without a reason.

Restlessly pacing the room, Julian thought back over the conversation. Suddenly, he stopped dead in his tracks as the realisation came to him that Bawtry's purpose had been to find out why he hadn't made inquiries when Lynne failed to keep the lunch date. He ought to have made inquiries, but he hadn't dared to risk going to the police. On the other hand, he had offered a reasonable explanation, hadn't he? Lynne had been prevented from coming by a business appointment, that was what he had thought. And he hadn't known of the bank raid and the abduction until after the show because he hadn't listened to the radio or bought a newspaper. He had done both those things — but nobody knew that, did they? He had answered this inspector's questions readily and reasonably. There was nothing to fear, nothing.

Just the same, the time was nearing when he must quit — get back to London or even leave the country, anything which would put him a long distance from Liverpool. He savoured the thought, liking its taste. Then other thoughts stirred. I can't leave, not yet. It might start something more than routine in this inspector's mind. I'll have to stick it out, at least until the case is closed. Why the hell don't the coppers pin all the bank raids on this man they've arrested? That's what I thought they'd do, he's the obvious suspect. Perhaps they *will* do that in the end? Meanwhile, I'll have to stick it out. They've nothing on me,

Nothing . . . That's right, they haven't — put on a bold front, keep a stiff upper lip, just carry on as if nothing had happened, and nothing had — nothing which links me with the other bank robberies.

Nothing . . . except the money, right here in this flat. Suppose Bawtry came back for whatever reason and started looking round? Don't panic, there isn't any reason why he should. Better if I hide the money somewhere else, though. But where? I could lock it in the boot of my car — no, that's probably the first place they'd look if things went wrong. But they're not going wrong, they *can't* go wrong. Better to take avoiding action, though . . .

The thought ceased as another came to him. An hour later he had rented a bed-sitter in the Liverpool 8 district, paying in advance. He gave his name as Mr. James Smith, lately of Rushholme, Manchester, and went there wearing one of the disguises he had used. He locked the big suitcase in the clothes closet, then locked the bedsitter up when he left. Now nobody could find the money.

He drove to a car park, changed out of the disguise and sat in the car for twenty minutes before driving out to the hospital to collect Lynne. A smile moved on his handsome face. Everything was going to be all right . . .

★ ★ ★

Another conference, a late afternoon one this time. Braxted in the chair, flanked by Ballinger and Fallon. Brooker in a corner chair, still dangling his hands between his knees, a small cigar gummed to his mouth. Bawtry sat facing the wide desk.

Ballinger said evenly: 'We have a series of first reports from the detectives assigned to the new inquiries. As we arranged, the briefing was to retrace their way over the original investigations but asking new questions in the hope of uncovering some fact or facts we missed the first time round.' He looked from one to the other, as if inviting comment. Nobody spoke.

'It was largely your idea, Bawtry . . . '

'Yes, sir.'

'And a good one,' said Ballinger. He fingered a sheaf of foolscap reports. 'I concede that despite the fact that so far the new inquiries have proved wholly unproductive.'

'May I see the reports, sir?'

'Of course.'

Bawtry skimmed through them. Brooker re-lit his cigar. Fallon re-charged a noisome pipe, looked sideways at Braxted.

'Smoke it if you must, Ted,' said the Detective Chief Superintendent resignedly.

Bawtry said: 'On a preliminary reading the inquiries simply bear out the first ones.'

'Also on a second or third reading,' Ballinger said.

'I'm sorry.'

'That's all right — going over the ground has been worth while as a process of elimination. Specifically, it would seem to eliminate an unknown bank raider, I think.'

Bawtry sat for a moment fingering his plain gold cuff-links. Finally, he said slowly: 'You think all the robberies were done by Tolman, sir?'

'I'm not saying it as an established fact, but I think the balance of probabilities points in that direction. I take it you don't agree, Bawtry?'

'I interrogated Tolman at length and in detail and formed the impression that he wasn't implicated in the earlier raids.'

'A hardened criminal like Tolman would lie his way out of anything, wouldn't he?'

'Yes, sir, he would if he thought there was a chance of getting off the hook — but there isn't. We have conclusive evidence substantiating charges of robbery, kidnapping and murder. More than enough to put him down on a life sentence. Tolman has nothing to lose by confessing to the earlier raids — on the contrary, an admission might mitigate the severity of the sentence.'

'I agree that's possible — but it could work the other way round. An admission of involvement in the previous robberies could earn him a longer term, depending on the view the judge takes.'

Brooker intervened. 'Tolman had the proceeds of the major raid in the condemned terrace house, but there was no trace of the earlier proceeds, sir.'

Ballinger sounded a little testy. 'I am aware of that, Brooker — but he could have concealed the money elsewhere, or have made it up into a parcel and posted it to another address, possibly an accommodation address in London. I gather that he comes from London.'

Fallon set fire to his pipe, using a desk blotter to hit dancing sparks. 'Tolman *could* have hidden the other money here on Merseyside — in some other place.'

'It could be anywhere.' This from Braxted. 'The point seems to be that we haven't found it.'

'I am aware of that, too,' said Ballinger. There was a small edge to his voice, which was unusual. 'I'd like us to make a renewed attempt to find it. Tracing a piece of stolen property is standard police procedure. Also, there will be fingerprints on it.'

Braxted looked up. 'Do you want Tolman re-interrogating?'

'I was about to suggest that.' Ballinger stood up. 'With no reflection on Bawtry I suggest that Brooker takes over this time.'

'Nobody to touch Sam at the old interrogation,' said Brooker stolidly. 'Not even me,' he added.

'I have the highest regard for Bawtry's talents in that direction, but a change of approach may do no harm. It may even produce something positive. I'll be in my office when you're through, Brooker.'

Bawtry said equably: 'Meanwhile, I'd like to go through the reports in detail, if you've no objection, sir.'

'None whatever, Bawtry.'

It took Bawtry forty minutes to read and re-read the reports. They yielded nothing he didn't already know. He put them back in their folder and sat thinking. He had the intuitive feeling that somewhere, just beyond immediate reach, was the way ahead, clearly signposted. The trick was to identify the signpost. It wasn't to be found in the painstaking reports he had just read, of that he was certain. He let his mind drift in the hope that, subconsciously, it would fasten on to something, however slender. Something like what? A lead — any kind of lead — which would bring him closer to the ringer who had executed the original series of bank raids. The ringer . . . the word came unbidden into his mind. A man who, if Bawtry's theory was correct, was a master of disguise, like an actor, a character actor. For God's sake, the only actor I know is Julian Arbor and he doesn't look like a blagger. On the other hand, a blagger didn't necessarily look like a blagger. It's too bloody ridiculous, though. Arbor didn't even know about the hold-up and the shooting and the abduction until late at night. Odd that he didn't do anything when Lynne Mayes failed to keep the lunch date, though. Or was it? It was a reasonable explanation that he supposed she had been detained by some unforeseen business commitment. You can't feel a man's collar for that. No, I'll have to look elsewhere. Where? I don't know. The ringer might be a couple of hundred miles from Liverpool by now, counting his loot, taking a holiday in Majorca, anything. Yes, he might; but he also might still be in the patch, holed-up in some inconspicuous flat, even a shabby bedsitter, biding his time until the heat went off.

Suddenly, Bawtry stiffened slightly. The only place the ringer had actually been seen in was the Liverpool 8 district. Bawtry reopened the folder and went through the reports yet again. No reference to Liverpool 8. The plainclothes d.c.s had seen everybody on the case except Joey Kalmar and Ronnie Albertson. Probably hadn't thought it mattered. Maybe it didn't, but . . .

The telephone rang. 'Call for you, Mr. B.,' announced the girl on the switchboard. 'It's being made from a public kiosk.'

'I'll take it.'

A voice said: 'Mister Bawtry?'

'Yes — who's calling?'

'It's me — Joey, Joey Kalmar. Look, I only put 2p in't box, so I'll have to be quick.'

'Go on, Joey.'

'I've seen him agen, not five minutes since — fella what left the bike. He had different gear on, but it was 'im for sure — the same thick hair and tinted specs, sunglasses like.'

Bawtry could hear himself breathing hard down his nose. 'Do you know where he went, Joey?'

'I followed 'im for a bit, up towards Myrtle Street, then he went down this entry and when I got there he'd gone. I'm sorry, Mister Bawtry, but I did me best.'

'When you grow up you'd better join the police force — you've done better than a squad of about fifty detectives. This entry — has it got a name?'

'Yeh, Blake's Yard it's called. I can't think where he went — it doesn't lead anywhere except round the back of a free car park. There were a couple of cars there, but they was empty. An old banger and a red Cortina . . . '

'And this was not much more than five minutes ago?'

'That's right . . . ' Joey paused, said excitedly: 'Hey, d'yer think he was making for t'car park?'

'Happen he was. Stay where you are, I'll be with you in quick-sticks.'

Bawtry literally ran into the police yard for his car. It was a short drive to Myrtle Street, but before he got there he made a detour which would bring him to the entrance side of the car park. He was almost there when a 1600 Cortina passed him, going the other way.

Julian Arbor was driving it . . .

Bawtry turned into the car park, really a dirt-surfaced demolition area. There was only one car on it, a clapped-out old banger, a 1966 Beetle. Nobody was sitting in it.

Joey came down the entry. 'Hi, Mister Bawtry.'

'I thought I told you to stay where you

were.' Not that it mattered.

'I guessed you'd be going to the car park and thought I'd come, too. Did you see 'im, then?'

'There wasn't anybody here, Joey.'

'He came down the entry, I seen 'im — he must've been and gone.'

'Yes,' said Bawtry.

He drove back to Police Headquarters. Brooker came up from the cells. His interrogation technique was a mixture of menacing charm and explicit antagonism. Sometimes it paid off — but not this time, Bawtry judged, looking at the hard seamed face.

Brooker said candidly: 'I tried to break him down, but no go. Tolman's sticking to it that he knows nowt about the other bank robberies.'

'And?'

'I hate saying it about a villain like Brad Tolman, but I think he's levelling, as the Yanks say.' Brooker grinned. 'That makes it two to one against Ballinger. He won't like it.'

'Ballinger's a good Deputy Chief Con., all the same.'

'Yes, he is — but he's wrong about Tolman, I'm bloody sure of it.'

'What about Braxted and Fallon?'

'I'm not quite sure where they stand — but, forced into a corner, I think they'd be on our side.'

'What was your private opinion before you saw Tolman in the cells?' asked Bawtry directly.

'Who, me? I had an open mind. No, that's not quite right. My inclination was to throw the book at Tolman — but the inclination was weakened by the line you took. And that's meant as a compliment.'

'The tribute is appreciated.'

'Mind you, I tried every trick I know to catch him out — but either he didn't betray himself or there wasn't anything to betray. I concluded it was the latter.' Brooker glanced up at the big wall clock. 'Time we weren't here, we've done enough for one day. Also, they've been open for the last hour. But I suppose you're going straight home?'

'I'll have a quick one with you,' Sam said. 'But first I want to make a phone call.'

'All right, I'll get them in while you make it. The pub round the corner in five minutes flat, eh?' Brooker picked up his hat and went out, with the resolute stride of a man about to start the serious business of the day.

Bawtry got the telephone directory up on the desk, found the number and dialled.

A remembered voice said: 'Julian Arbor speaking — who's calling?'

'Bawtry here.'

'Good evening, Inspector. You're lucky to catch me in. Another five minutes and you wouldn't have — I'm just about to go down to the theatre. What can I do for you?' The tone was suave, but inside him Julian was aware of a renewed sense of unease.

But Bawtry's next words dispelled the sensation.

'I don't think you can do anything for me, Mr. Arbor. I'm just ringing up to let you know that we're now working on the theory that Tolman, the man in custody, was responsible for the previous bank robberies.'

206

'Oh, really?' Julian tried to keep the jubilation out of his voice, but something of it reached Bawtry.

'I thought you'd like to know — particularly as you put forward the same idea when we met earlier. You're in good company — the Deputy Chief Constable endorses that view.'

'Well, thanks indeed for telling me, Inspector.'

'No trouble. I was going to ring you this afternoon, but it occurred to me that you might be out.'

There was the smallest pause. Then Julian said: 'It would've been all right — I've been in all day, as it happens. But thanks again.'

'That's all right. By the way, how is Miss Mayes?'

'She's fine, I'm happy to say. I'm taking her up to the Lakes for a short holiday — I've a week off coming up. Next week, as a matter of fact.'

'That should do her good, particularly if the weather stays like it is. Give her my regards.'

'I'll do that.'

Bawtry let the receiver slide back on its rest. He stood there for a long moment, looking at it without seeing it. He could still hear Julian's voice saying: 'It would've been all right — I've been in all day as it happens.'

But he hadn't . . . and the fact of it made him a liar.

Why?

There had to be an answer.

14

'Thought you weren't coming, Sam,' said Brooker amiably. 'There's a pint waiting for you.'

Bawtry would have settled for a half, but he didn't say it.

He picked up the tankard, not yet drinking from it. Eyeing him, Brooker said: 'You've something on your mind.'

Bawtry grinned faintly. 'I didn't know I was making it so obvious.'

'You aren't — but I know you and I can always tell, well, nearly always. What's up?'

Bawtry drank some of the bitter, put the tankard down and said slowly: 'When I re-read the reports I noticed that the d.c.s hadn't bothered to see the kids in the Liverpool 8 district. They retraced all the ground, with this one exception.'

'Likely they didn't think it would be productive — the kids had already told you about seeing the fella with the secondhand bike. The d.c.s did go back to the dealers, though — probably decided that was sufficient. If you think it important we can send them up to Liverpool 8.'

'It doesn't matter now, Brook.' Bawtry rarely used the diminutive version of Brooker's name and when he did it slightly embarrassed him. Mostly, he avoided addressing the Detective Chief Inspector by any name. But he knew that Joyce Wetherby called him Brook because she didn't know his given name and Brooker wouldn't tell her. In fact, it was Eugene — a name which Brooker, though not an introspective man, intensely disliked and which Bawtry couldn't bring himself to utter.

Brooker said evenly: 'Why doesn't it matter now?'

'I decided to see these kids again myself — but before I could do it one of them, young Joey Kalmar, came on the blower. He said he had just seen the fella who ditched the bike — wearing different gear, as he put it, but with the same thick greying hair and sunglasses.'

'No actual shortage of fellas with thick hair and tinted specs these days — was he sure it was him?'

'Quite sure.'

'What did Joey Kalmar do next, then?'

'He followed him.'

Brooker's face creased in a grin. 'Sounds like he has the makings of a cop.'

'That's what I told him.'

'What happened?'

'The man went down an entry called Blake's Yard. By the time Joey had got down it the man had vanished.'

'Fella can't simply vanish in thin air.'

'This one did, or Joey thought he did. The entry doesn't lead to another street, it comes out at the back of a cleared site used as a car park, or available as one. I doubt it's used much.'

'Any motorist leaving a car in that area's liable to come back and find the wheels missing — probably the engine as well. What did young Kalmar do?'

'He went to the nearest phone box and got through to me.'

'What did you do?'

Bawtry lit a cigarette, blew the match flame out and said: 'I ran for my car and drove there at once. I thought there might just be a chance that I'd spot someone answering to the description.'

'But no such luck?'

'No, I didn't see anyone with thick hair and sunglasses. Instead, I caught a passing glimpse of a man I know, driving a red Cortina 1600. He didn't see me — the way he was going he had the sun in his eyes.'

'What man?' Brooker asked gently.

'An actor named Julian Arbor — he's with the repertory company at the new Riverside Theatre.'

'I didn't know you numbered actors among your acquaintances, Sam.'

'I don't, but I know Julian Arbor — he's a friend of Lynne Mayes.'

Brooker peered at his cigar as if half-expecting to surprise a guilty secret. 'You're warming up to something, Sam. I don't know what it is, but you are.'

'The day Lynne Mayes was kidnapped she was supposed to meet Arbor for lunch. Well, of course, she didn't turn up — or more accurately, she couldn't.'

'What did Arbor do — call the police, is that how you come to know him?'

'No . . . he didn't do anything until late at night when he went to see her in hospital. He said he thought she had been detained by business and that he didn't hear about the bank raid and the abduction until after the show at the Riverside.'

'Well, it's possible . . . ' Brooker paused. 'Or are you thinking of something else?'

'I wasn't, not at the time — though I thought it, well, unusual. Enough to call on him.'

'And you accepted his explanation?'

'Well, yes — though I still thought it odd.'

'And then you see him driving back from the Liverpool 8 district?'

'That's right.'

'I still don't see the point. Why shouldn't he be driving there?'

'No reason. I simply registered the fact that he was driving towards the city centre in a red Cortina 1600.'

'Sam — you're taking your time over this, aren't you?'

'Yes, but it's necessary to establish the full picture. Well, I drove on and found the car park. It backs on Blake's Yard. It isn't really a designated car park — just a cleared site and is hardly ever used, for the reason you mentioned just now. The only car on it was a right old wreck which looked as if its owner had dumped it there. Then Joey came down the entry and I asked him if there were any other cars on this land when he followed chummy.'

'Well?'

'Joey said he saw another car — a red Cortina.'

Brooker started violently, spraying cigar ash. 'Christ!' he said.

Bawtry went on levelly: 'Joey said there was no one in the car — or, rather that he didn't see anyone in it.'

'If there *was* somebody in it he'd have noticed, surely?'

'He'd be bound to — unless whoever was in it had slid down out of sight.'

'Did you think he had?'

'Not at first — but now I'm pretty sure of it.'

'Why?'

'Something happened, or I made something happen. After I left the car park I drove straight back to Headquarters and rang Arbor, ostensibly to tell him we were now working on the theory that Tolman committed all the bank raids — which was what he had suggested when we met.'

'As good a way of opening a conversation as any — but by now you had something else in mind?'

'Yes. I wanted to ask if he'd been to the car park, but I judged it better to adopt an indirect approach. I had the feeling that I'd have been showing too much of my hand and that he would automatically disclaim all knowledge of the place.'

'But you did something.'

'I set a trap — a small one, but still a trap. I said I had meant to ring him earlier in the afternoon. For a second he didn't answer — *then he said he had been in his flat all day.*'

'He didn't have to say that — he could simply have passed it off.'

'He could — but he didn't and that's the point.'

Brooker's hard blue eyes flickered briefly. 'What you're saying is that it was a reply designed to disarm any suggestion that he was at the car park in a red Cortina, even though you hadn't actually made that suggestion?'

'Yes.'

'What you are also saying is that Arbor is the blagger who pulled off all the other bank jobs.'

'I'm not yet saying it as a fact, but as rather more than a probability — perhaps even that a *prima facie* case exists.'

'And all this began because you thought it odd that Arbor didn't start anxious enquiries when his girl friend failed to turn up for lunch?'

'In a sense, yes — though I didn't consciously suspect him at the time. I just thought it funny peculiar. At that stage it wasn't anything more than a subconscious feeling that there was something wrong about it — but young

Joey Kalmar remembering having seen a red Cortina on the car park changed things.'

'Suppose Arbor had simply said yes, I've been out this afternoon?'

'I'd have been stumped or I'd have to have tried something else. But he didn't. He lied — and that was a mistake because, unless he had something to hide, it didn't make sense.'

Brooker jingled coins in his trouser pocket. 'We've no proof, you know that.'

'Yes. What's your view?'

'I think Arbor requires investigation.'

Bawtry caught the barmaid's questioning eye. 'Two small Scotches,' he said.

Brooker grinned. 'You're setting me on the hard stuff, and that's not good — once I start I'm liable not to know when to stop.'

'I was under the impression you could handle it. I've never seen you under the influence.'

'I'll tell you a secret, as we used to say in my boyhood — I'm adept at masking the symptoms. As a matter of fact, though, I hardly touched the stuff, or any other kind of drink, until after Marion walked out on me.' Brooker made a sound that was less than a laugh. 'I've made up for it since. I thought, when I took up with Joyce, that she might object to me having a whisky breath — but she likes the stuff, too. But she knows when to stop.'

Brooker paused. Then: 'Am I right in thinking that before young Kalmar came on the blower you were going out to Liverpool 8 anyway?'

'Yes.'

'What for?'

'It occurred to me that whoever did the earlier bank jobs might well be living there — or, alternatively, might have rented a flat there.'

'As a hiding place for the stolen money?'

'I thought it was a possibility. Then I saw Arbor driving and that made me change tactics.'

'If Arbor and chummy are one and the same he could have the money at his proper address — or at some convenient address in Liverpool 8. He could've used the deserted car park to put on and take off his disguise — keeping down out of sight while he did it . . . '

'We've no knowledge that he has a place there.'

Brooker drank some of his whisky and breathed out through his mouth. 'It's not too late to find out. I know an agent who has the letting of small properties converted into bed-sits — I'll ring him now. Hang on a tick.'

He crossed the bar and wedged himself in a public phone box. He was back in a few minutes. His face wore an animated expression.

'We're in luck. I caught Jim Bennett just as he was about to go out. He says the most recent letting was a bedsitter in Ackroyd Terrace — to a fella with thick greying hair and sunglasses who gave the name of John Smith from Rusholme, Manchester, and paid in advance. Number 5 Ackroyd Terrace, room six.'

'The description fits . . . '

'We won't need a warrant — acting on suspicion that the place is being used

219

for the concealment of stolen property. Besides, we won't have to force a way in — Bennett's leaving a pass-key with his missus.' Brooker made a dry chuckle. 'This mucks up my night's drinking and your personal arrangements.'

Bawtry finished his drink and said: 'I'll phone Carol that I'm likely to be late home. It won't be a new experience for her,' he added ruefully.

'She shouldn't have married a cop — least of all a C.I.D. jack,' said Brooker. His eyes flickered briefly. 'If we find the money there we've got him . . . ' He paused. 'Wait a minute — have we?'

'Only if we can prove that he *is* the man who rented the bedsitter. He'll deny it and, as he went there in disguise, the chances are that neither your friend Bennett nor anyone else can positively identify him.'

'Still, getting hold of the stolen property is more than half the battle,' Brooker argued.

'Yes, but it's not enough. Ideally, we should walk in while Arbor is there, in person . . . ' Bawtry stopped.

Brooker said nothing, eloquently.

'What we have to do is induce Arbor to be on the premises first.'

'How?'

'Another trap,' said Bawtry.

★ ★ ★

Julian had gone to the bedsitter to help himself to more than enough money for a holiday with Lynne. He hadn't been aware that Joey was following him, hadn't seen Bawtry driving and when Bawtry came on the phone with the news that Tolman was now the sole suspect for all the bank robberies he was jubilant.

Now he was fully in the clear. Everything was going for him . . .

15

By the time Bawtry arrived at the theatre
the curtain was coming down on the first
act. Don Perry, who was in the foyer,
came up.

'Detective Inspector Bawtry?'

'That's right.'

'You don't know me but I know you,'
Perry said amicably. 'Or, rather, I saw
your picture in the evening paper and
recognised you. I'm Don Perry.'

'Happy to make your acquaintance,
Mr. Perry.'

'You here on business or to see the
show?'

'Just a passing visit.' Bawtry liked
the look of Perry, but at this stage
he wasn't disposed to be more than
non-committal.

Perry said: 'I'm a member of the
repertory company. Usually, I'm on stage
but for this week I've been promoted
— not sure that's the right word — to

stage director. Can I buy you a drink?'

'If you insist,' smiled Bawtry.

'We have quite a nice cocktail bar,' Perry said. He led the way in. 'Large Scotch?'

'A small one, I think.'

Perry signalled to the barmaid. 'A couple of wee whiskies over here, Mabel.'

The drinks came. Perry raised his glass and said: 'A toast is in order, I think — you've solved the bank robberies and rescued the girl who was abducted, I gather.'

'We had a certain amount of luck on the way.'

'Well, one needs that over most things — it's what you do with it.'

'Once we knew where Miss Mayes had been taken, it was straightforward.'

'Julian Arbor was telling me that you've got the man responsible for all the raids.'

'We have a man in custody, a professional bank robber named Tolman. He's been charged — but so far only with the latest raid.'

'Oh? Julian seemed to think he's being charged with all the raids. He mentioned that you had been on the phone to him about it.'

'I did tell him that we were working on that theory — but we haven't finally excluded the possibility that another man or men may be implicated in the earlier crimes. We'll see.'

Perry fiddled with his glass. Bawtry who was acutely perceptive to nuances of behaviour, sensed that he was preoccupied about something.

Finally, Perry said: 'If it's not an impertinent question — what made you contact Julian?'

'It was just a passing call, like coming here tonight. We had information that he had a lunch date with Miss Mayes, but she didn't keep it. I thought he might be worried. Actually, it turned out that he concluded she had been held up by an unexpected business commitment — in fact, he apparently didn't know she had been kidnapped until late that night.'

'Yes, we were going to have a drink together when the news came through that she was in hospital, so he dashed out there.' Perry hesitated, as if he was about to say something. Instead, he picked up his glass again.

Bawtry looked at him, then said quietly: 'Is something troubling you, Mr. Perry?'

'Why, should there be?'

'I don't know, but you look as if something might be. Is it?'

Perry turned an inscribed signet ring on the third finger of his left hand. He seemed to be trying to make his mind up. Finally, he said: 'It's something I noticed in Julian's dressing-room after we had the news that this man Tolman had been arrested and Lynne Mayes had been rescued.'

'What was it you saw, Mr. Perry?'

'A copy of the evening paper. It was on Julian's dressing-table. It was folded in half on the front page — open on the story about the raid and Lynne Mayes being kidnapped. I just thought it odd.'

'He may have bought the paper and folded it open without actually reading it,' said Bawtry. It wasn't what he thought, but it would do.

'I didn't think of that.' Perry looked relieved. 'Yes, of course, that could be

225

it. Only I thought . . . ' He didn't finish what he was saying.

Bawtry didn't try to do it for him. Instead, he said: 'The evening paper didn't carry the story of the arrest because it didn't happen until later. And when Arbor heard that he at once went to the hospital?'

'Yes, he did. He was very concerned. I just thought it was funny the newspaper being on his dressing-table — it didn't occur to me that he hadn't read it. But, of course, that must be it.'

'If he had read it he'd have been worried much earlier in the day, wouldn't you say?'

'Yes, of course. I ought to have thought of that.' Perry glanced at his watch. 'If you're seeing the rest of the show please regard yourself as our guest, Inspector.'

'I bought a ticket on the way in, but thanks for the offer,' Bawtry said. 'The curtain will be going up again in a few moments — I'll find my seat. And thanks for talking to me.'

Bawtry found his stalls seat and watched the rest of the play, noting

Julian's expertise in playing three markedly different rôles. He took three solo curtains before the entire company appeared for the final one.

Don Perry was in the foyer as Bawtry came through. 'Hope you enjoyed the play, Inspector.'

'I found it extremely interesting. By the way, I have a small piece of additional information for Mr. Arbor. I take it I can go backstage?'

'Assuredly. I'll show you the way.'

Julian was removing his make-up. He looked round as Don Perry announced: 'Inspector Bawtry to see you, Julian. If you'll both excuse me, I have to be at the front of the house.'

Bawtry closed the door and said: 'First, congratulations on your performance, Mr. Arbor — or perhaps I should say performances. Not an easy thing playing three major rôles, I imagine.'

'You were in the audience, then?'

'Yes, I enjoyed the play immensely.'

'Kind of you to come backstage and tell me, I'm sure.'

'I had another reason, Mr. Arbor.'

'Oh?'

'Yes. As you know, we're working on your own theory that Tolman may have committed all the bank robberies. But there's a development. We arrested Tolman in a condemned terrace house up near the docks — but we now also think he had another place as well.'

'Really?'

'The proceeds of the earlier bank raids weren't in the condemned house. It occurred to us that he may have used a second address as a hiding place.'

'I suppose that's possible,' Julian said. He made the words sound casual.

'We think it is.' Bawtry paused, letting a long silence hang in the still air.

Julian lit a cigarette. He had to fight to keep his hand steady. 'Well, that's quite a development, isn't it?' he said. 'I take it that you haven't yet located this other address?'

'Not yet, but we think it may be in the Liverpool 8 district.'

Julian went rigid.

Bawtry said equably: 'We're getting a list tomorrow of all recently let flats and

228

bedsitters there. With a little luck we ought to be able to trace the place.'

Julian breathed out audibly. 'Tomorrow, eh? I wish you luck, Inspector.'

'It may take a little time, but we'll locate it in the end. It occurred to me that you'd be interested in view of your theory about Tolman.'

'I am indeed — and thanks for taking the trouble.'

Bawtry smiled. 'I was in the theatre just as one of the audience, but it struck me you'd like to know the latest development, Mr. Arbor. We should know if there's anything in it sometime tomorrow. Well, I'll be going.'

Julian held out a hand. It was cold again.

★ ★ ★

Bawtry had parked his Rover 2000 in a side-street. He turned it round and stopped just short of the stage door entrance. The wait wasn't more than minutes. Then Julian came out. He walked fast to the mouth of the dead-end street and flagged down a cruising taxi. Bawtry trod gently on the accelerator, followed at a discreet distance.

The taxi stopped at the block of city centre flats. Julian paid it off and went in. This time the wait was longer. Bawtry used the time to put the Rover out of sight in a pool of blackness created by a short line of tall trees.

Finally, a figure came down the steps, rapidly. A man with heavy greying hair and sun glasses. He got a crimson Cortina 1600 out of a lock-up garage and started driving.

Towards the Liverpool 8 district . . .

Bawtry hung back, far enough behind to see without being noticed. Not that keeping the Cortina in sight really mattered, because he knew where Julian was going. Into the trap. The bedsitter ringed by police with Brooker in the control car. For Bawtry the procedure would be simple: park just short of 5 Ackroyd Street, walk in, using the pass-key if necessary, and confront Julian in possession of the loot. If he makes a break for it don't worry — he'll run slap into the cops.

Bawtry was nearly there when the Rover sagged, the steering going woolly. A blow-out, the front nearside tyre. He bumped to a stop, got out and started running. Two streets to go. He didn't see any squad cars, simply because they were deliberately keeping out of sight. *Somebody* ought to see *him*, though.

He turned into Ackroyd Street, counted the way down to No. 5. No red Cortina outside, nor any car. No lights on in the bedsitter, either. But Julian had to be there, inside — nothing else made any sense.

Bawtry went up four aged-rounded steps, the kind diligent housewives used to donkey-stone in days long gone. Bawtry reflected that by now the police must have seen him, slightly puzzled because he was on foot. But they wouldn't act until he gave the signal — three flashes from a powerful hand torch. He found the bedsitter and tried the door. It didn't yield. He used the pass-key and stepped in, feeling the wall for the light switch. He

231

found it and thumbed it down. Nothing happened. He stood totally still for a moment while his eyes adjusted to the darkness.

A thin current of air riffled towards him from the rear window. It was wide open and creaking, off the ratchet.

Suddenly, he knew what had happened. Arbor had been and gone, staying just long enough to lift the money — then out the back way through the window — aided by the blow-out. He must have left the Cortina somewhere round the back of the property. Bawtry stood by the window, looking and listening. Nothing. He crossed the room to the front window and flashed the torch three times. Then he went back to the rear window. Fire escape stairs led down to a dirt yard. The Cortina was there, concealed by the black shadow created by the overhang of the high wall, waiting — but not for Julian Arbor. By now he had gone, merging into the deep shadows of a small maze of cobbled alleys where the squad cars wouldn't be; weaving his way on foot, lugging a suitcase wadded with a fortune in stolen banknotes. He must have spotted the waiting jacks, or some of them, and abandoned his car because they wouldn't be looking for a man on foot.

Police were swarming in now. Brooker shouted: 'Sam — where are you?'

'Down here at the back . . . '

'Where's chummy?' Brooker asked the question as he thudded down the fire escape.

'Gone!'

'We didn't hear any car . . . '

'He left it down here.' Bawtry pointed as Brooker joined him. 'He must've spotted one of the police cars and made off down the alleys on foot.'

'He'll not get far.'

'I'm not so sure — he's got a start on us and we don't know which way he went, there's half a dozen alleys round here.'

Brooker bawled orders. 'Search these alleys — split up into pairs and go through them with a bloody tooth comb.' Brooker paused. 'Saw you come running into the street, Sam — what happened to your car?'

233

'Blow-out. It gave Arbor just enough time to get away.'

'Sod it,' said Brooker. 'We'll catch up with him, though.'

Bawtry said meditatively: 'Any one of these alleys will get him clear of the area.'

'Happen they will, but a fella humping a suitcase is conspicuous . . . '

'My guess is he'll hail the first taxi that comes in sight . . . '

'Not back to his flat — not with all that money. He daren't go there. More likely he'll have the cabbie drop him off, miles from here. No, that doesn't add up — we'd find him just the same.'

'Not if he's gone to Lime Street station, catching the first train out — to anywhere.'

'Christ,' said Brooker. 'That'll be it! Come on.'

They went there in a squad car, siren wailing, straight through the traffic lights — any colour. Several trains were alongside platforms, waiting.

Bawtry said: 'The London train's in — he'll have made for that.'

They went to the barrier. The ticket collector, who knew Bawtry, said: 'Hello, Mr. B. — something up?'

'We're looking for a man who may have boarded the London train in the last ten minutes or so . . . '

The collector grinned. 'A lot of people have got on it — what's he look like?'

Brooker said tersely: 'Tall fella, about six feet, probably wearing thick grey hair and sunglasses.'

The collector blinked. 'How d'you mean, probably wearing thick grey hair?'

'It could be a wig,' Brooker said impatiently.

'I don't remember anybody like that, but there were a lot got on the train, like I said, and I didn't notice them all . . . ' He paused. 'Wait a minute, there was one tall fella with dark hair, carrying a suitcase, just the one. He wasn't wearing sunglasses — but he had a pair sticking out of his breast-pocket. He didn't have a mac — I noticed that and thought it funny, going on a train journey without a mac, what with the weather being uncertain.'

A following squad car came up. Brooker said: 'You lads get on every train. Question every man on board, looking specially for a man with no raincoat. Inspector Bawtry and myself will join the London train — you take the others.'

The collector said: 'You haven't time to buy tickets . . . '

Brooker grinned. 'Sue us!'

Bawtry glanced down the long platform. 'Can we have the train held while we search?'

'If you'd been a few minutes earlier you could, but there's no time now — the departure's just been signalled.'

Bawtry didn't answer. They went past the collector, who called: 'T'fella had a first-class ticket — that ought to help.'

'Thanks, it does,' Bawtry shouted back as they yanked open the first door. The train was already moving.

Brooker said: 'Well, we've done it — we can't get off this side of Crewe.' His leathery features creased. 'But neither can chummy. Meanwhile, all we have to do is stroll through the first-class coaches submitting one and all to a pitiless scrutiny.'

An off-duty dining car attendant stood aside to let them pass.

Bawtry said: 'Are all the first class coaches at the front?'

'Yes, sir.'

'No dining car or buffet at this time of night, I suppose?' asked Brooker.

'No, sir.' The attendant hesitated, then said: 'Excuse me, but are you two gentlemen police?'

'The descriptions don't necessarily tally, but you've got it right first time. How did you guess?'

'I just thought you might be. Business?'

'You could say that. We're looking for a man in his middle thirties, about six feet tall, who got on the train carrying a suitcase but not wearing or carrying a raincoat. Your colleague at the barrier said he had a first class ticket.'

The attendant screwed his eyes up as if trying to recall, but finally said: 'No, can't say I saw him — but I've been busy. What's he done — robbed a bank?'

'You're in good guessing form,' Brooker told him.

They went down the train to the first class section. Brooker said: 'You do the looking, Sam — you know Arbor.'

Bawtry nodded. They moved slowly to the front of the long train. Nobody looked like Julian Arbor.

'He isn't here,' Bawtry said.

'Dammit — he must be!' Brooker paused. 'Unless he saw us arriving and got off as we got on . . . '

'It's possible . . . '

'Wait a minute — he could've spotted us and then shut himself up in one of the toilets.'

'We'll try them,' said Bawtry.

There were four lavatories, in pairs. Three were showing the *Vacant* sign, but they looked inside just the same. The fourth was engaged. Brooker rapped on the door, said loudly: 'Police — we'd appreciate a word with you.'

There was a small pause, then a voice — an agitated feminine voice: 'How dare you come knocking — can't you see it's engaged?'

Brooker coloured. It was the first time Bawtry had ever seen him looking embarrassed.

'Sorry, ma'am . . . '

'I should think so . . . go away!'

'Please accept our apologies,' Brooker said. He turned to Bawtry. 'Is my face red?'

Bawtry grinned faintly. 'A little.'

'Hell, I never thought of a woman being in there. What do we do now?'

'Try the second class coaches — we went through them without bothering to look, though I'd have expected to see him if he was there.'

'He could've had his head well down or pretending to read.'

'Happen . . . ' Bawtry sounded doubtful.

'If he's not in the first class fella must be in the second.'

'In which case he'll know we'd come back. Well, we can try.'

They went back through the coaches. Brooker stopped. His hard face wore a baffled look. 'He's not on the train, Sam!'

Bawtry didn't answer.

'He must've got off at Lime Street and we didn't see him. There's no other explanation . . . ' Brooker stopped. His light blue eyes, hard as agates, were riveted on Bawtry. 'Now what.'

Bawtry said slowly: 'Something just struck me — Arbor is an actor, an expert at making himself up. He's also an expert at disguising his voice.'

Brooker started violently. 'For God's sake . . . '

'We heard a woman's voice from the bolted lavatory. If Arbor's on the train it's the only place where he could be — we've searched everywhere else.' Bawtry had already started back along the train.

Behind him Brooker said: 'Sam — you've got to be right, unless he did get off.'

'We'll find out, one way or the other.'

The train began to slow down. They were within sight of the last of the toilets when the door to it started to open inwards and a man came out, sideways because of the suitcase he was carrying. He turned his head to glance down the train and saw them. His face was a ravaged mask.

'Arbor!' Bawtry shouted the name.

They were still a small distance from him. Bawtry started running as the train juddered to a stop. The arrested motion threw him forward, staggering.

Julian was wrenching at the exit door. He stood there for a second, swaying, like a travestied ballet movement.

Bawtry shouted again, 'Don't do it, Arbor — don't do it. There's a . . . ' He lunged ahead as he spoke, reaching out with both hands.

But Julian was already leaping through the wide open door, in the path of an oncoming train.

'*Christ*!' said Brooker.

The suitcase spun from Julian's hand, ahead of him in a high arc. It hit the grass embankment, rolled down to the edge of the track. They found it when the oncoming train had passed — undamaged.

They also found what was left of Julian Arbor. Only his gold watch and his driving licence told who he was.

16

The inquest and the funeral were both over and Brad Tolman was in Walton jail awaiting trial at the next Crown Court.

Bawtry looked up from his desk as a uniformed constable announced: 'Miss Mayes to see you, sir.'

She came across the floor and gave him a long slim hand.

Bawtry, who had risen, said smilingly: 'This is an unexpected pleasure, but how did you know I was in?'

'I didn't, I just took the chance. I felt I had to see you . . . '

'Yes?' He drew up a chair for her.

'I came to thank you for what you did — trying to stop Julian jumping from the train.'

'If I'd guessed that he was in the toilet a few moments earlier I'd have been in time to stop him.'

'You tried — Sam.' She hesitated, then said: 'Do you think he knew the other

242

train was approaching?'

'I think he did — and took the risk, believing he could just make it.'

She shivered.

'I don't think it was suicide, Lynne.' Bawtry fingered his cuff-links. 'But it wasn't worth risking his life — he would probably have got away with a three-year sentence.'

'That would have been frightful for him, though, wouldn't it? Despite what he did he was really a very gentle kind of person.'

'Yes, prison isn't a nice place to be in, no matter what you may hear to the contrary.'

'It would have been especially bad for a man like Julian. He wasn't a hardened criminal, he was just an amateur. That's another reason why I've come . . . I wanted you to know that he wasn't really bad.'

'I'm sure he wasn't Lynne.'

'I think he must have seen himself as a sort of modern Raffles — you know, getting away with all that money and laughing at authority.'

'He very nearly did have the last laugh — in fact, he would have done but for one thing, the sixth raid — the one he didn't commit.'

'I'm not sure I quite follow that . . . '

'He thought Tolman would be the sole suspect for all the bank raids.'

'*You* didn't think so,' Lynne said quietly.

'No. Tolman was a killer as well as a bank robber — but when he denied knowledge of the other raids I believed him. Also, I couldn't rid myself of the feeling that there was something odd about Julian's claim that he didn't know you had been kidnapped. But, even accepting that, it seemed strange that he made no inquiries when you failed to turn up for the lunch date.'

'So you went to see him — questioned him?'

'Yes. Even then he could have got away with it — but when I saw him the second time he told a completely unnecessary lie. I asked a question, but the question itself was a trap and he fell into it.'

'And that was enough?'

'Not by itself. To be certain I set a second trap.' Bawtry told her about it.

She said: 'Julian walked right into that one, didn't he?'

'Yes — though I couldn't forsee the result. It never occurred to me that he'd jump from the train.'

'I suppose it was an impulse — the jump for freedom.'

'Yes. But he wouldn't have got away even if the other train hadn't been coming — we'd have caught him.'

'Would you have still set the trap if you'd known another train was approaching?'

'That's a hypothetical question,' said Bawtry.

He walked with her to the main entrance of Police Headquarters. A five-year old Hillman Hunter was parked outside. Don Perry was in it.

'I think you know each other,' Lynne said.

'Yes. I didn't know you were acquainted, though.'

'Don called to see me after it happened . . . we became friends from the start. I hope you don't think that's wrong of me.

You see, I wasn't in love with Julian, not really in love, so . . . so it seemed all right.'

She made a small laugh. 'The nicest thing about men is that they're all the same,' she said enigmatically.

When Bawtry went home he repeated the words to Carol. She said: 'That's a sensual cynicism. There are other factors. Men *are* different.'

Bawtry grinned. 'What makes you say that?'

'Because I know one who is,' answered Carol.

THE END

Other titles in the Linford Mystery Library

A LANCE FOR THE DEVIL
Robert Charles

The funeral service of Pope Paul VI was to be held in the great plaza before St. Peter's Cathedral in Rome, and was to be the scene of the most monstrous mass assassination of political leaders the world had ever known. Only Counter-Terror could prevent it.

IN THAT RICH EARTH
Alan Sewart

How long does it take for a human body to decay until only the bones remain? When Detective Sergeant Harry Chamberlane received news of a body, he raised exactly that question. But whose was the body? Who was to blame for the death and in what circumstances?

MURDER AS USUAL
Hugh Pentecost
A psychotic girl shot and killed Mac Crenshaw, who had come to the New England town with the advance party for Senator Farraday. Private detective David Cotter agreed that the girl was probably just a pawn in a complex game — but who had sent her on the assignment?

THE MARGIN
Ian Stuart
It is rumoured that Walkers Brewery has been selling arms to the South African army, and Graham Lorimer is asked to investigate. He meets the beautiful Shelley van Rynveld, who is dedicated to ending apartheid. When a Walkers employee is killed in a hit-and-run accident, his wife tells Graham that he's been seeing Shelly van Rynveld . . .

TOO LATE FOR THE FUNERAL
Roger Ormerod

Carol Turner, seventeen, and a mystery, is very close to a murder, and she has in her possession a weapon that could prove a number of things. But it is Elsa Mallin who suffers most before the truth of Carol Turner releases her.

NIGHT OF THE FAIR
Jay Baker

The gun was the last of the things for which Harry Judd had fought and now it was in the hands of his worst enemy, aimed at the boy he had tried to help. This was the night in which the past had to be faced again and finally understood.

MR CRUMBLESTONE'S EDEN

Henry Crumblestone was a quiet little man who would never knowingly have harmed another, and it was a dreadful twist of irony that caused him to kill in defence of a dream . . .

PAY-OFF IN SWITZERLAND
Bill Knox

'Hot' British currency was being smuggled to Switzerland to be laundered, hidden in a safari-style convoy heading across Europe. Jonathan Gaunt, external auditor for the Queen's and Lord Treasurer's Remembrancer, went along with the safari, posing as a tourist, to get any lead he could. But sudden death trailed the convoy every kilometer to Lake Geneva.

SALVAGE JOB
Bill Knox

A storm has left the oil tanker S.S. *Craig Michael* stranded and almost blocking the only channel to the bay at Cabo Esco. Sent to investigate, marine insurance inspector Laird discovers that the Portuguese bay is hiding a powder keg of international proportions.